Duel at Del Norte

Russ Wikeley settles in the boom town of Del Norte, South Dakota, hoping to erase the memory of a sordid past. After foiling a bank robbery he is persuaded to stand for sheriff in the forthcoming elections. However, a scheming gang boss by the name of Diamond Jim Stoner wants his own man to become sheriff and when he discovers Russ's secret he is quick to spill the truth.

Stoner's plan backfires but he refuses to give up that easily. Not to be thwarted in his plan to take over the town, Stoner hatches a new scheme to frame his adversary for robbery and murder.

Will Stoner's dastardly plan succeed? And is Russ prepared to lie down and play dead? Both men are full of determination . . . but only one can be the victor in the final duel on the streets of Del Norte.

Duel at Del Norte

Ethan Flagg

A Black Horse Western

ROBERT HALE · LONDON

© Ethan Flagg 2010
First published in Great Britain 2011

ISBN 978-0-7090-9035-9

Robert Hale Limited
Clerkenwell House
Clerkenwell Green
London EC1R 0HT

www.halebooks.com

Typeset by
Derek Doyle & Associates, Shaw Heath
Printed and bound in Great Britain by
CPI Antony Rowe, Chippenham and Eastbourne

ONE

ELECTION FEVER

Russ Wikeley was sweeping the boardwalk fronting his photography shop. He paused, leaning on the broom, then sniffed the air. It was a weather forecasting ploy he had learned from an old Cheyenne medicine man.

'Another hot one, Russ?' commented Dewlap Jenson, the owner of the town's only news sheet. A cheeky smile indicated that he had every confidence in the photographer's uncanny ability.

'Maybe so until mid-afternoon,' observed Russ seriously, his perceptive proboscis twitching. 'Then we're in for a flash storm.'

Jenson shook his head. The fleshy jowls that had given rise to his nickname quivered with perplexity.

'I don't know how you do it, Russ,' he muttered.

The photographer winked coyly. 'Trade secret, Dewlap.'

Since the discovery of a new gold seam at the north end of Blacktail Gulch, the *Del Norte Tribune* had upped its circulation and now operated as a double-page spread. Advertising had also doubled. With every day that passed, new prospectors were flooding into the Black Hills hoping to make their fortune. Most were destined for disappointment. Only the lucky few ever struck real pay dirt. But that didn't stop them trying.

Most headed for Deadwood. But the recent strike outside Del Norte had upped the small town's profile.

The increased population was a mixed blessing.

On the one hand, stores and mercantiles were enjoying greater business. Russ had seen his own trade boom in recent weeks as successful miners poured in, eager to have their pictures taken showing off the all-important lucre.

But prosperity had its down side.

More noise, fights and arguments over claims. Not to mention carpetbaggers! Those parasites always appeared where a new source of pay dirt had been discovered. Russ was well aware that once the easy pickings had disappeared, the boom would end as miners moved on to the next discovery. The townsfolk would then be left to pick up the pieces.

The once beautiful valley was being rapidly laid bare as miners stripped its coating of pine trees. Stretching well up either side of the vaulted slopes, only the stumps now remained.

'Morning, Russ.'

The harsh tone of Betsy Harding's discordant voice

fitted well with her starchy demeanour. Wife to the town's medic, the close-set eyes and birdlike features gave her thin frame the appearance of an ill-fed chicken. Russ could never figure what the attraction had been for the easy-going doctor. The two were like chalk and cheese. Perhaps that was it. Opposites attract.

Although it was towards their daughter that Russ had cast his net. How such a starchy specimen could be the mother of such an elegant creature was beyond his cognizance. Eleanor Harding was a light in the wilderness of the drab gold-town. A lustrous gem shining through the murky waters of greed that were now suffocating the old settlement.

Russ doffed his hat, acknowledging the greeting with a friendly bow.

'Who are you voting for in the election?' asked Betsy. A haughty sniff was accompanied by a wagging finger. 'Not that lackey backed by Jim Stoner, I trust.' The probing beady eyes challenged him to disagree.

Diamond Jim had come to Del Norte ostensibly as a land speculator. He had then proceeded to buy up all available vacant lots, upon which he had erected saloons catering to the insatiable demand for rest and relaxation from the mining fraternity. Where once there had been a single watering hole on Alder Street, there were now five.

All owned by Diamond Jim Stoner.

Already he had bought out the store adjoining Russ's Studio. And Kee Fong's Chinese laundry on the other side had mysteriously burned down only the previous week. Russ had refused point blank to sell his own premises. He knew that Stoner wanted the triple site to build a music-hall theatre. No way was he going to be buffaloed into kowtowing to the arrogant speculator.

'Ain't made my mind up yet.' Russ chose to adopt the middle ground. His stony gaze focused on the Panhandle saloon above which were located the suite of rooms occupied by the shifty toad.

For the last two weeks all talk had been centred on the upcoming election of the new law officer for Del Norte.

The present incumbent had realized that he was just not up to the job any more. Ben Stockley was well past his best. An unhealthy taste for hard liquor and Ma Plumbake's steak pies had slowed his reactions. Retirement had been forced on him by circumstances. Truth was, he could no longer effectively control the streets of Del Norte. A tough new lawdog was needed.

In his younger days, the sheriff had been the scourge of boom towns from California to Montana. The name of Wild Ben Stockley had struck fear into lawless elements who unwisely chose to call him out. His name had gone down in the fighting annals of the frontier as the man who single handedly tamed the lawless town of Bannock back in the '60s.

It was even rumoured that the old guy had been forced to buy a new revolver, as the old one having fallen apart due to the number of notches cut into the rosewood butt.

But that was then.

The Del Norte of 1878 was just as mean, but Ben Stockley had run out of steam. The wild streak of yesteryear had fizzled out like a damp firework. The vegetable patch he cultivated on the banks of Blacktail Gulch was now a far more enticing option.

'There aren't that many choices when it comes to electing a new sheriff,' observed Dewlap Jenson. Then, turning to Mrs Harding, he added, 'I'm with you on the unsuitability of Cimarron Charley Newcombe for the job. The guy's nothing but a two-bit gunslinger brought in by Stoner to guard his back and help fleece the honest citizens of Del Norte.'

'So who are you gonna vote for?' asked a curious Russ Wikeley.

'Only other fella in the running is Brad Craven.'

Russ remained tight-lipped. A deal of scepticism was written across his face. Stockley's deputy had only been in the job for three months. Sure he could handle a gun. But it needed guile and cunning as well as brawn to police a frontier town. Craven was nought but a greenhorn. He lacked the experience necessary for running a boom town and the surrounding territories.

Betsy was about to voice her opinion when gunfire erupted from down the street. The town was no stranger to the discharge of firearms. But not at this early hour on a Monday morning.

In the front room overlooking Alder Street above the Panhandle, Diamond Jim was adjusting his cravat. He was a well-built dude. Thick black hair slicked down with pomade was neatly trimmed.

And taking centre stage was the enormous glittering diadem that was his trademark. Like a vigilant eye, it winked in the early morning sunlight that beamed in through the open window.

Jim Stoner considered himself to be a businessman, an entrepreneur. Not to mention a handsome dude about town. Tall and debonair, the gang boss cast an admiring glance in the mirror. He was well pleased with the clean-cut profile reflecting back at him. With nonchalant aplomb, he casually flicked an imaginery speck of dust from the shoulder of his tailor-made black suit.

He possessed a wicked charm that intrigued a certain type of female. The sort that frequented saloons. But he professed no interest in those. It was toward the medic's daughter that his ambitions focused.

Diamond Jim wanted to become *respectable*.

Gone were the days of being a two-bit hired gunslinger. On the run, always looking over your shoulder, one step ahead of a pursuing posse. That was now all in the past.

He cast a disdainful glance towards the hard-boiled accomplice lounging idly in the corner. Let the hired help do all the dirty work now. Jim Stoner was here to rake in the rewards and let others take the rap.

'You should have just chased that darned clothes-scrubber out of town,' Stoner admonished his confederate. Then, with a cutting bite of mordancy, added, 'instead you had to skewer his guts with that pig-sticker.'

Charley Newcombe bit his lip. He wasn't used to taking a dressing-down, being treated like a schoolkid. His grip tightened on the ten-inch Bowie picking at his long finger nails. The hired gunman hailed from Cimarron, New Mexico. Wildest town in the territory, and Newcombe had always been in the thick of the action.

That was until the Pinkertons arrived to clear the town of its reckless elements. Cimarron Charley judged it prudent to quit town and head north. The newly opened goldfields of South Dakota would doubtless afford good prospects for a man of his talents.

And so it proved.

When he shot dead a cheating cardsharp on his first night in Del Norte, Jim Stoner had immediately put him on the payroll. That had been two months before. It was easy money. Collecting rent from storekeepers, and persuading miners that Diamond Jim's assay office payed the best price – less a fat commission, of course. In fact, once the other assay office in Del Norte had mysteriously closed its doors, Stoner's was the only one left.

'Crazy Chink started squealing and hollering like a scalded cat,' countered Newcombe with a suitably owlish glare. 'He woulda wakened up the whole town if'n I hadn't pinned his yellow hide to the floor.'

Diamond Jim scowled. 'I had to pay out good money to keep that killing under wraps,' he snarled.

'If it had been a whitey, that old has-been Stockley would never have taken the bribe.' He wagged a threatening finger at the burly tough. 'You just be glad we were able to get rid of the body and make the fire look like an accident.'

Newcombe stiffened. His black eyes narrowed to thin slits below the heavy brows.

His response spat out with menacing intent. 'Nobody speaks to me like that,' he hissed. Pausing for effect, his right hand slowly dropped to the low slung gun butt on his hip. 'Not even you, Jim.'

Stoner's waxed moustache twitched, the smooth cheeks assuming a reddish hue. He hated the hired help calling him by his first name. But the slippery jasper also recognized that Charley Newcombe was a vital part of his overall plan. For now he would have to grin and act the part of a contrite equal. It rankled. With the greatest effort, Stoner summoned up a tight smile. Thin lips drew back as he replied.

'Take it easy, Cimarron,' he mollified in a condescending tone of voice while handing a cigar to the bodyguard. 'We gotta maintain a respectable front if'n you're to become sheriff with me appointed as the new mayor.'

Then with false bonhomie, he chuckled, 'Once we've gotten our feet firmly under the table, this town will be ours for the taking. And with all them miners wanting to ship their pokes through here, just think of the commission to be made.' He slapped the gunslinger heartily on the back. 'And that's just the start. Stick with me and you'll be a rich man inside of a year.'

12

Gunfire down the street stanched any further conversation. And it was coming from outside the bank.

Stoner grimaced. This was the last thing he wanted.

TWO

ROBBERY

The three acquaintances flung curious glances towards the source of the fracas. What in thunder was going on? They didn't have long to wait.

Three men had emerged from the bank. Each was clutching a grey sack. A fourth was holding their mounts ready for a quick getaway.

One of the robbers turned and loosed off a couple of shots at a man who had just emerged from the bank. It was the teller and he was holding a small Deringer. A foolhardy act for a greenhorn desk-johnny, which earned him a lead sandwich. Throwing up his arms, the bank employee fell to the ground, blood pumping from a fatal chest wound.

'The bank's been robbed!'

The strident cry from Betsy Harding stunned the others into silence. But only for a brief instant.

'Inside!' snapped Russ, grabbing a hold of the

woman's arm and pushing her into the studio. Jenson was left open-mouthed, apparently in shock. This was the first time he had witnessed such an overt display of disorder since starting up the newspaper.

Once he had ushered the two people inside the studio, Russ grabbed a hold of the rifle he always kept ready under the counter. It was well-oiled and fully loaded. He jacked a round into the breech.

'And keep your head down, Betsy,' Russ exhorted the doc's spouse as he hustled out on to the boardwalk.

Positioning himself in the middle of the rutted street, legs firmly astride, he jammed the rifle into his shoulder. Then, displaying careful deliberation, he sighted along the barrel. Sharp ears picked up the muted rumble of panic-stricken voices from down the street as the four robbers viciously spurred their mounts in his direction.

'Let's get outa here, boys,' hollered a bluff jasper waving his six-shooter and loosing off at the bank's windows to deter any other potential heros.

Del Norte lay at the head of a boxed-in gulch. And this was the only escape route. Whooping and hollering with delight at having pulled off the heist, they pumped lead at any unfortunate citizens who displayed an excess of curiosity. Splinters of glass from a dozen shattered windows was enough to keep heads down.

Tense laughter pursued the flying bullets.

So intent were the hold-up men on keeping the citizens pinned down that they failed to heed the lone man blocking their escape. Before they realized what was happening, the throaty roar from Russ's Winchester had emptied the saddles of half their number.

'Haul up or eat dirt, you sons-of-bitches!'

The brittle command found the two remaining outlaws desperately trying to bring their frightened mounts under control as their two sidekicks bit the dust. Startled faces glanced right and left. But there was no way out of the trap into which they had blundered.

The bearded leader uttered a manic growl of anger when he perceived that only one man was blocking their escape.

'You're the one who'll be chewin' lead, mister,' he yelled, raising the heavy Colt. The gun was never fired.

A third bullet lifted the big man out of the saddle. He was dead before his body hit the street. The rifle immediately swung to cover his confederate. But Arby Duggan had seen enough. His gun hit the dust, both hands reaching skywards.

'OK, mister,' he hollered. 'You've got the drop on me. Don't shoot. I surrender.'

When they realized that the gun battle was over, people began emerging from cover. Voices were raised in excited chatter as the action was played out again. And each time the telling grew more vivid.

Russ was immediately surrounded. His back received a pounding from numerous animated onlookers.

'Boy, that was some shooting,' commented an old-timer.

16

'Never knew you had it in yuh,' from a second.

'How does a durned photo-snapper get to be so good with a gun?'

This last query brought puzzled looks from the gathering throng.

'Who cares?' piped up another. 'He stopped the bank being robbed, didn't he? And that's all that matters.'

That was the general view. Most of the spectators were running claims up the gulch and had their pokes deposited at the town's only bank.

At that moment a small plump man elbowed his way through the thick mass of bystanders. He was sweating copiously, having run all the way from the bank. Homer Doubleday was the manager.

'The bank is most grateful for your timely intervention in preventing a most dastardly hold-up, Mr Wikeley,' he wheezed, mopping his bald head with a handkerchief. 'I am sure that the trustees will be more than generous in rewarding your enterprise.'

Russ's eyes clouded over.

'I didn't do it for no reward,' he protested. Then, in a more subdued tone, he enquired, 'How's the guy that was shot?'

The manager's face adopted a suitably mournful expression. He shook his head. 'I regret that poor Mr Cropper is. . . .' He swallowed. 'I'm afraid he didn't make it.' Then his round face brightened. 'In the meantime, to celebrate the subverting of this heinous crime, everyone is welcome to join me over at the Red Rooster.'

'Who's payin'?' queried a dubious voice from the rear.

'Why, the bank, of course.'

A raucous cheer erupted at this announcement. Within seconds the assembled throng had dispersed towards the more than welcome pursuits offered by the Red Rooster, leaving Russ alone in the middle of the street.

Death comes easy to a boom town, he mused pensively.

He was quickly joined by Betsy Harding and Dewlap Jenson.

The newspaperman guessed what they were both thinking.

'Why don't you put yourself up for the sheriff's job, Russ?' Jenson suggested.

Betsy nodded her agreement.

'No!' snapped Russ, rather too abruptly. 'I'm a photographer, not a lawman. Anyways, I wouldn't know where to begin.'

'But we need someone the town can rely on to serve our interests,' the woman persisted. 'And you're head and shoulders above the other candidates.'

'And you clearly know your way around a gun,' added Jenson, a puzzled frown crossing his angular face. 'Where the heck did you learn to shoot like that?'

Russ shrugged off the compliment. This was a road down which he did not wish to venture.

'Only from hunting with my pa when we lived in Kentucky.'

Before the others had chance to pursue the matter further, Ben Stockley wandered up. Russ heaved a gentle sigh of relief.

'Bit late aren't you, Sheriff?' muttered Jenson. 'All the fun's over.'

Stockley huffed some before blurting out a less than adequate excuse for his tardy arrival.

'I was otherwise engaged at the far end of town,' he said.

'Watering them dog-daisies, I'll be bound,' scoffed Betsy Harding.

'As a matter of fact it was official business,' countered the lawdog, trying to reassert some degree of authority. 'Anyway, I'll need you to come down to the office,' he said addressing Russ. 'To give a statement.'

Russ was more than happy to depart with the ageing lawman in the company of their despondent prisoner.

'Give our hero some legal tips while you're about it, Ben' shouted Jenson to their backs. 'Seeing as how he's gonna be our new sheriff.'

A rat-faced jigger lurking in the shade of the overhanging veranda quickly hustled off down the street. Known simply as Laramie Joe, he was a swamper and general dogsbody at the Red Rooster. The little weasel knew that Jim Stoner would fork out good drinking money for such a choice titbit of information.

It was later that day, and Stoner was only just recovering from the bleak realization that funds he had counted on for buying up some land on the edge of town were now in jeopardy. For it was he who had hired the gang of robbers to hold up the bank. They had been brought in from Pine Ridge, south of the Badlands. The idea had been for Newcombe to meet up with them at Cheyenne Crossing for the pay-off and to take charge of the loot.

He hadn't counted on that meddling skunk Wikeley thwarting his plans. Who'd have believed that a picture-popper could handle a gun like that? There was clearly more to Mr Russell Wikeley than met the eye.

Now three of them were dead and one of the muddle-headed critters was in jail. If Arby Duggan squealed to save his miserable hide, Diamond Jim Stoner would be up the creek in deep water. To forestall this eventuality, he had sent one of his men, a young hardcase know as the Kansas Kid, over to the jail to persuade Duggan where his best interests lay. The Kid was Stoner's latest recruit.

'Who is it?' rapped the gang boss, lurching to his feet. Beads of sweat clung to his brow. Waiting on the Kid's return from his visit to the jail was making him edgy.

The door opened and a pair of foxy orbs peered at him. It was Laramie Joe.

'Got some news for yuh, Mr Stoner,' muttered the swamper nervously.

The gang boss ground his teeth.

'It better be good,' he snarled, aiming a rabid glare at the intruder. 'I'm busy. Can't it wait?'

'I figure you'll want to know this.'

'Go on then,' rapped Stoner, puffing hard on his

cigar. 'Out with it.'

Laramie breathed deep. 'Russ Wikeley is running for sheriff. I just heard his buddy, Dewlap Jenson announcing it to the whole town. So you can bet on it being front page news in the *Tribune* tomorrow.'

Newcombe visibly stiffened at the news. He had reckoned on a straight-aces win in the election race. The deputy was just a kid. Handy with a gun maybe, but no competition for a hard-boiled rannie like Cimarron Charley Newcombe. A dark glower, brooding and laced with unease, clouded the gunman's weathered visage.

This new entrant in the race was a dark horse. And he could be a different proposition altogether. If Charley had been informed of the photographer's intentions yesterday, that really would have been a joke. But in view of Wikeley's bold and bloody handling of the bank robbery, the guy had proved he had the nerve, not to mention the prowess with a rifle.

Stoner was no less concerned.

This piece of information would need careful handling. Both the mining fraternity and the regular townsfolk would throw their weight behind the photographer. The election and job of sheriff was his for the taking if something wasn't done to stymie the notion.

A frigid silence descended over the morose gathering.

It was the shifty rodent who broke in on the grim reflections.

Gingerly he asked, 'Isn't that worth knowing, Mr

Stoner?' The whine in his voice got under Diamond Jim's skin. But he recognized the need for employing rats like Laramie Joe to keep him informed.

With snappy disdain, he flicked a silver dollar at the fawning weasel.

'Now get out!' he snapped.

The door slammed shut leaving the two confederates in a saturnine mood.

'Don't think on it, Cimarron,' growled Stoner acidly whilst arrowing a harsh glare at the furious gunman. Charley Newcombe was checking the load of his ivory-handled Colt Frontier. 'That's your answer to everything, ain't it? A bullet in the back. This needs to be done legit.'

The all-important question was how? At the moment Jim Stoner had no answers. He paced the room. Heavy lines of frustration creasing the handsome features were equal to those of his confederate.

But Stoner had the benefit of an agile and devious brain. That was why he was in charge, and Newcombe was merely the hired help. And he would need every bit of his cunning and guile to figure out an angle that would checkmate this threat to his lucrative plans for Del Norte.

Minutes passed slowly. An urgent knock was a reminder that the Kansas Kid had returned.

The young gunslinger swaggered in through the door.

'Is he gonna play ball?' rapped Stoner.

'Duggan reckons you owe him,' replied the Kid, lighting up a cheroot. He aimed a plume of blue smoke at the ceiling before continuing. 'He figures you should help him to escape and throw in a grub-stake.'

'Does he now?' growled the prickly gang boss.

'I could plug him,' suggested Newcombe, giving a lurid smirk. 'Easy as falling off a log. Just stick this here hogleg through the back window and. . . .' He aimed an imaginary gun at the hovering messenger. 'Bang! Bang! You're dead!'

'Don't you ever learn.' Stoner wrung his hands in frustration. He was surrounded by dumbclucks. 'That would tell the whole darned town that somebody here had planned the robbery,' he crowed derisively. 'And we all know who the fingers would point to.' He jabbed a thumb at his own chest. 'An escape is the only answer. That way nobody here will be implicated.'

THREE

COYOTE BOB RAMONE

The studio was about to close up for the night when Russ walked in.

'You can go home now, Elmer,' he called to his assistant.

The photographer had been taken up with matters connected with the robbery. And not merely providing a statement to the sheriff. Numerous grateful citizens had delayed him with offers of free drinks, not to mention the bank manager insisting on buying him dinner at Ma Plumbake's diner.

Throughout the afternoon, exhortations to stand for sheriff kept assailing his ears from all sides. By the time Russ had reached the studio, the constant pressure had almost persuaded him that it was the right and proper thing to do. But there were still some

24

nagging doubts.

Russ Wikeley and the law had not always seen eye to eye. But that was behind him, another world far removed from his current situation. And that was how he wanted it to stay.

'Yeah. Thanks, boss.'

Elmer just stood there, his jaw hanging wide. Staring eyes fastened on to his employer. This was a totally different person he was seeing since the gun battle. Russell Wikeley the diffident photographer had suddenly changed into a dime-novel hero.

'No need to stare, Elmer,' chided Russ, concealing a smile.

'S-sorry, b-boss,' stuttered the boy, reluctantly dragging his eyes away from his new paragon. 'Folks are saying that you might be running for sheriff. Is it true?'

'Ain't decided yet,' replied Russ, handing over the plates that he had taken of the bank robber now languishing in the town jail. 'Get these plates processed first thing in the morning.' He had no wish to discuss the delicate matter with his employee.

The curt avoidance of the issue, however, was no deterent to the apprentice who persisted with his enquiry.

'Every single customer this afternoon has said that you oughta stand,' pressed the youth earnestly. 'We've had a heap of miners wanting their pics taken. And they all reckon you're the ideal fella to protect their interests.'

'And I second that.'

The lilting cadence effectively curtailed the snappy response Russ was about to make. He spun on his heel to face the ravishing creature who had quietly entered the premises. The dark outline of Eleanor Harding's profile silhouetted in the doorway emphasized her shapely contours.

The effect was mesmerizing and stunned both Elmer and his boss into silence.

Every time Russ saw her, Eleanor's bewitching allure intensified. Her golden tresses glinted in the sunlight. She tossed them with carefree abandon, fully aware of the effect she had on men. A flawless complexion, smooth and unblemished by the harsh environment, made the hero of the hour nervous and twitchy. And the velvet dress only served to accentuate the emerald coolness of her piercing green eyes.

They had not exactly been walking out together. A picnic, a couple of turns round the floor at the monthly barn dance, was all. And last week, a ride out to the Flying V stud ranch to look over the stock. Doc Harding had promised to buy his daughter a new horse for her twenty-first birthday.

Russ was pleased she had seen fit to ask him to help make the choice of a mount. But he knew that the next move was up to him. The thought of asking such a comely flower to step out with him was a more unnerving proposition than facing down a dozen bank robbers.

'Well?' Fully aware of her spellbinding effect, Eleanor stepped inside the studio. 'Cat got your tongue, Russell Wikeley?'

Only his mother and this girl had ever called him by his full name. It sounded strangely erotic issuing from those rouged lips.

'Just thinking, Elly,' he mumbled sheepishly.

'If Charley Newcombe and Brad Craven are the only pair in the running,' she told him, 'then you have to stand. Pa's always saying that the town needs a strong pair of hands to guide it along the right tracks. I always knew you were good with a rifle when it came to hunting deer and rabbits.' She paused to emphasize her enhanced admiration for this unlikely hero. 'But what happened today has turned you into the town's saviour.'

'That's just what I've been telling him,' interjected Elmer Todd.

'It's your bounden duty to stand now, don't you think?' The girl underlined her statement with flickering eyelashes. Hands resting on rounded hips, her challenge was irresistible.

Russ stroked his blunt chin. The matter was fast moving beyond his control. If he stood any chance with this girl following the day's events, he had no choice but to register his candidature.

'Well,' he drawled a touch hesitantly. 'I guess so.'

'That's it then,' she said breezily, clapping her hands. 'We'll go down to the council offices straight away and sign you up.'

Arm in arm, they hustled along the boardwalk, the girl more than willing to bask in her paramour's glory.

From a window on the far side of the street Jim Stoner jealously watched their progress. Daggers of hate flashed at the strutting pair. Amorous designs of his own involving Eleanor Harding looked to be in jeopardy before they had even started. This critter was becoming a thorn in his side. He slammed a balled fist into the wall.

'There's not a man alive who's gotten the better of Diamond Jim Stoner,' he growled under his breath. 'And no damn blasted store clerk is gonna be the first. You picked the wrong man to tangle with, mister.'

A rancid glare pursued them down the street, then Stoner turned round.

'Everything ready for tonight?' The waspish snarl was aimed at Newcombe.

The gunman nodded. 'I'll wait until after midnight when the town's settled down. Shouldn't be any problem dropping a pistol through the barred window at the back. Kansas has already primed the prisoner on what to say when he gets the drop on the sheriff.'

'You mean about telling the old soak that a sidekick slipped him the shooter?'

'That's right,' agreed Newcombe. 'Everybody will then reckon it's an outside bust and leave us in the clear.'

'We still have to deal with this guy Wikeley,' Stoner pointed out. 'There has to be some means of stitching him up.' A malicious glint of determination stole across his pinched visage. 'And I intend to find it.'

Next morning the town was abuzz with news that the jailed bank robber had escaped. Rumours abounded as to how it had occurred. Ben Stockley had

28

been discovered at first light by the cleaner. Bound and gagged, then locked in one of his own cells, the old guy had been released and escorted to the town clinic.

It was only after Doc Harding had judged him sufficiently recovered from the ordeal that the truth had emerged.

Naturally the shamefaced lawman tried to play down the fact that he had been negligent in his duties. How was he to know that the varmint had a gun hidden away? The fellow had hoodwinked the custodian into thinking he was sick. Sometime after midnight, Stockley had been woken by the prisoner calling out in pain. When he had entered the cell-block, the guy was rolling on the floor clutching at his stomach.

Being a kind-hearted sort of guy, the sheriff had naturally opened up the cell and gone to his aid, only to have a six-shooter jabbed in his ribs.

When he asked the guy how he had managed to get hold of the gun, it had emerged that a confederate was in on the rescue. He had been hidden out in a draw to the north of town.

Then the thankless dog had slugged him, leaving him trussed up like a Thanksgiving turkey. Stockley rubbed his bandaged head.

'Sooner I can retire the better,' were the old guy's parting words as he headed for the nearest saloon. Nobody disagreed with him on that assertion.

Stoner couldn't resist a sly smirk at the retreating back of the discredited lawman. That was one problem sorted. Now all he had to figure out was a means of turning the tables on that blasted photographer.

It was two days later. The church clock had just struck two in the afternoon.

Lightning crackled in the sky above the scalloped moulding of the western crags as yet another storm threatened to deluge the town. Spring in the Black Hills was always a time of rain and more rain. Flash flooding often brought the movement of goods and people to a complete standstill. Deep ruts filled with water made the negotiation of Alder Street a hazardous undertaking.

Although the storms rarely lasted for more than a half-hour, it could be very frustrating. Such was the burden of digging for gold in the Black Hills. But for most, it was a price worth paying.

In his office, above the Panhandle saloon, Jim Stoner was pacing the floor. Unbeknown to the arrogant speculator, the answer to his dilemma concerning Russ Wikeley had just paused at the southern limits of the town.

Saddle tramp was an apt description for the shabby rider hunched over the neck of an equally down-at-heel mustang. Perusing the signboard, he slowly mouthed the legend thereon.

'Del Norte – elevation: 2455 feet, population: 2576.' The previous count had been scrubbed out. A brittle cough, meant to ressemble a laugh, issued from beneath a thick bushy moustache. 'Somebody musta had twins recently.' The horse ignored the comment, continuing to chew on a clump of grass.

The man lifted his gaze to the ugly cluster of wooden buildings stretching away along this bottom end of Blacktail Gulch. A pair of furtive eyes peered out from beneath the battered slouch hat.

Everything about his appearance spoke of a man down on his luck: scuffed boots, a soiled grey shirt and a weathered face that had not seen a razor for upwards of a week. To the casual observer he would appear to be just another no-account drifter on the scrounge.

That is unless you took heed of the well-oiled gunbelt complete with its nickel-plated Colt Peacemaker. Such a rig implied an owner able and experienced in gunplay. Like a wounded grizzly, he was someone to be given a wide berth.

Coyote Bob Ramone nudged the mustang back into motion.

He had come north to the Black Hills after hearing of the gold strike, although the gunman was not interested in the yellow pay dirt. More to his liking were the less arduous peripherals that usually accompanied such discoveries. And Coyote Bob knew that Del Norte would be no exception. The backbreaking toil of hard-rock placer mining was for suckers. Ramone was confident that hiring his gun out to one of the speculators who likely flourished in this boom town would once again find Lady Luck sitting on his shoulders.

Rumours had come down the grapevine that a certain Diamond Jim Stoner was the biggest operator in town. A simple enquiry informed him that the said gent occupied the upper floor of the Panhandle saloon.

'Third drinkin' den on the left,' remarked a bearded prospector. Bob's appearance was not unusual in Del Norte, and was no less dishevelled than the speaker's. 'A trio callin' themselves the Blacktails will be entertaining at this time of day. Yuh cain't miss it.'

The gunman nodded his thanks before dismounting. He tied his mount to one of the hitching rails and stepped up on to the boardwalk. And he was only just in time. Huge droplets of rain had been threatening for the last ten minutes. Suddenly, the heavens opened unleashing a full-blown torrent that proceeded to hammer the veranda roof into submission.

Coyote Bob flipped open a sack of Bull Durham, expertly rolled a stogie and stuck it between his lips. The lazy action allowed him time to survey the untidy burg as other travellers sought shelter. Sauntering up the street in the direction indicated, Bob Ramone's probing gaze missed nothing.

He had not taken more than five steps when a poster caught his eye. On closer inspection it proved to be an election advertisement. Nothing unusual in that until he laid eyes on the photograph of the prospective candidate. Bob's jaw dropped open. Could it be? He took a closer look, squinting to draw the picture into sharper focus.

Quickly his hand reached inside the back pocket of his faded blue jeans and removed a crumpled sheet. He opened it out, and laid the paper up against the poster for comparison. The guy on the election poster was more clean-cut, but Coyote Bob could have sworn it was the same man.

He hooked out the stub of a pencil and sketched a moustache and hat on to the poster. Dark brooding eyes popped when he realized that it was indeed the same man.

Staring back at him was none other than Blackfoot Reno Wixx, the killer of Bob's brother. He had been on the varmint's trail for over two years. The rat had changed his handle to Russ Wikeley. Same initials even. Quickly he read through the election blurb and drew the obvious conclusion that the killer was attempting to conceal his past under a cloak of respectability. And as a blamed photographer. The concept elicited a bitter laugh.

Well, Coyote Bob Ramone would soon bury that notion, bury being the operative word – in boot hill!

The gunman unflicked the hammer thong and loosened the revolver in its holster. He stamped off along the boardwalk, piercing eyes searching for the Magic Eye Picture Studio. Bob Ramone was good and mad, and itching for a showdown.

'This is where it's payback time, Reno,' he muttered under his breath. 'Prepare to be called out, you son of Satan!'

But common sense quickly slowed his pace. Stopping in front of the third saloon, he decided that a drink was called for to mull things over. No point causing himself unwelcome grief. He had waited two years already.

He swung through the batwings, and elbowed up to the bar. Bob cast a languid eye over the long, narrow room. In the far corner the Blacktails were giving an enthusiastic rendition of one of the latest ditties. A serious card-game was in full flow judging by the heap of dollar bills festooning the green baize.

But of the nattily dressed Jim Stoner there was no sign.

'What'll it be, stranger?' enquired the bartender.

Bob emptied his pockets. All he could afford was a small beer. The 'keep eyed the shabby trail bum with haughty disdain as he slid the foaming brew along the bar.

Bob ignored the offensive sneer. He had other things over which to ponder. He moved to the end of the bar, his dirt-smeared face creased in thought.

Blackfoot Reno, or Russ Wikeley as he was now known, was clearly well thought of in Del Norte. And a stranger suddenly arriving in town and gunning down their candidate for sheriff would, like as not, find himself the object of a lynch mob. Any claim of Bob's regarding the critter's unsavoury past would receive short shrift and be judged the ravings of a jealous rival.

However, a big shot like Diamond Jim Stoner carried more influence. He would surely welcome the opportunity to upset his opponent's law-enforcement ambitions. By raking up the guy's scandalous past, the way would be wide open for his own incumbent to pin on the tin star. And reward Coyote Bob for his opportune revelation.

Bob slung down the rest of his beer and slammed

the pot on the bar top.

'Tell Diamond Jim that he has a visitor,' he said to the supercilious barman. 'I have somep'n to tell him.'

The snooty barman peered down his stubby nose at this piece of dog manure cluttering up his bar.

'And what would an important citizen of Mr Stoner's calibre want with someone like. . . .' The 'keep responded with an arrogant sniff to underscore his revulsion for this offensive specimen. 'Like you!'

Bob Ramone might have been down on his luck. His stubbly face hadn't seen a bar of soap in a week. And his boots were leaking. But nobody talked to him as if he were the town drunk. Least of all some pompous toady of a beer-puller.

In the time it takes to say *Draw!* Bob's .45 was jammed up the bulbous snout. He grabbed the porcine lump's necktie and squeezed, yanking him forward across the bar top.

Sudden and violent, the altercation had not gone unnoticed. The card players turned as one. Drinkers shifted their gaze away from half-emptied glasses. The music faltered. All ears pricked up trying to hear what the fracas was about.

Bob's gritted teeth hissed out a brief message inaudible to the attending throng.

'You tell Mr Stoner that Coyote Bob Ramone wants words.' The gun pressed the cold steel harder, forcing the 'keep's head back. Quivering like a bowl of jelly, the guy's breath spewed out in short gasps, fear making him sweat buckets. 'And make no mistake, dog turd, he'll definitely want to hear what I have to say.'

35

Bob roughly pushed the barman away.

'Now git!' he snapped.

Trying to recover some lost dignity, the guy puffed out his pudgy chest like a preening bullfrog.

'T-take over, Mick,' he mumbled to his colleague, 'while I go speak with the boss.'

Waddling up the stairs as briskly as his rotund form permitted, the barman could feel Coyote's probing eyes drilling into his back.

Within minutes he appeared back on the upper veranda.

'The boss will see you now,' he burbled. Then with some spirit he added. 'But he ain't pleased at having his staff manhandled. So you best not be wasting his time.'

As they passed on the stairs, Bob affected the roar of a mountain lion, causing the barman to recoil. A lurid grin cracked the gunman's hard features. Sauntering along the upper corridor, confidence oozed from grubby pores. What he had to offer Jim Stoner was bound to reap dividends.

Then he could think about removing the skunk who'd shot down his brother, and claim the reward. And with the backing of the law, he surely held a winning hand.

FOUR

AMBUSH

The creature that stood before Jim Stoner was nothing short of a drifting hobo, a scrounger, just as his nickname implied. What could such a unkempt vagrant have to offer him? Jim Stoner was on the verge of having him kicked out on to the street where he belonged. Something held him back.

Cimarron growled.

'Want me to eject this bag of shit, Jim?' He didn't wait for an answer. A firm hand grasped hold of the man's grubby vest.

A barely audible hiss emerged from the man's gritted teeth. 'Lay another finger on me, and it'll be your last move.' The intense gaze that accompanied the warning was like a slap in the face to Charley Newcombe. His hand dropped to the gun on his hip. Nonetheless, he relinquished his hold.

Stoner had likewise taken heed of the stranger's

assured stance, and the accompanying aura of menace. Well versed in the analysis of human nature, he immediately sensed that Coyote Bob was no lick-spittle groveller. A brief gesture waved the bodyguard away.

'Let's hear what Mr Ramone has to say,' he coun-selled in a mollifying tone indicating to the visitor that he should say his piece. But an equally mean-eyed stare informed Bob that his health would be in serious jeopardy should the message prove less than satisfac-tory. 'And it better be good. Charley here don't take kindly to being threatened.'

Ramone smiled. It loomed more like an evil grimace as he reached into his saddle-bag.

'Take a look at this,' he said, laying the crumpled Wanted dodger on the desk facing Stoner. The boss eyed the paper. He shrugged impatiently. The name of Blackfoot Reno meant nothing to him.

A twisted scowl marred his handsome features. 'What's this got to do with me?' he rapped.

Holding the guy's challenging gaze, Ramone then laid the altered election poster beside it. 'Now take a closer look,' he said evenly. 'And tell me they ain't the same guy.'

Intrigued, Charley Newcombe had sidled over to scan the two sheets. He couldn't resist a brittle jibe.

'Umph!' he exclaimed. 'Who you tryin' to kid, mister. Ain't no way they're the same guy.'

But Jim Stoner was more circumspect. Dark eye-brows met in a pensive frown as he bent down for a closer view.

Then his eyes widened as the penny dropped.

'This fella's right,' he observed with a new tone of respect. The dark cloud lifted. Jim Stoner had found his opponent's Achilles' heel. His eyes glittered with renewed fervour. He jabbed a finger at the smiling face staring back at him from the poster. 'Gotcha, Mr Russ Wikeley.' Then with a harsh guffaw he added, 'Or should I say Mr Blackfoot Reno, wanted up in Montana for murder.'

'And it was my brother who he gunned down,' snarled Ramone.

The comment failed to register with the gang boss. His attention was cemented to the visual evidence for which he had been searching.

'So was it worth it?' prompted Ramone.

Stoner dragged his gaze back to this most welcome of informers. Sliding around the edge of his desk, he slapped the visitor on the back.

'Couldn't be better,' he averred, pouring out two slugs of best Scotch whisky. 'This is just what I need to finish off that varmint's political ambitions in this town once and for all.' They clinked glasses. 'I could sure use a man of your abilities.' Stoner grinned. 'Stick with me and you'll go places. This town is ripe for the picking, if you know what I mean.'

'Sure do,' replied Bob, grasping the man's proferred hand. 'Be glad to accept your offer, Mr Stoner.'

'Call me Jim. And once this guy's in the can, you can collect that reward.' The boss was in a buoyantly generous mood. 'I suppose you can use that hogleg?' he said, nodding to the fancy rig. In the blink of an eye the shooter was palmed and the two glasses on the desk had been shattered into tiny fragments.

Within a half-minute three men had slammed into the room, guns drawn enquiring as to the source of the ear-splitting roar.

Jim Stoner quickly recovered his composure following the sudden display of the gunman's prowess.

'Nothing to worry about, boys.' He laughed a little too loudly while attempting to soothe their worried glances towards the origin of the gunplay. 'Meet Coyote Bob Ramone. The newest recruit to Stoner Enterprises. As of now, he's on the payroll.'

Charley Newcombe was seething. He could see his status as the boss's right-hand man dissolving before his envious gaze. But he was damned if he would surrender without a fight. He left the room with the others. There was a bottle with his name on it behind the bar. It was about get a hammering.

Coyote Bob had made a vengeful enemy.

The sun was rising over the eastern rim of Antelope Creek when the two riders reached Cheyenne Crossing.

'What's this job the boss is so anxious for us to complete?'

Bob Ramone's query was aimed at his partner. It was two days later and the duo were riding abreast up the gentle gradient. The narrow pine-fringed draw had suddenly opened out at the pass. Twisted limbs of greasewood and stunted juniper relieved the flat terrain.

The task in question had been planned for over two weeks. Cimarron Charley had selected Ramone for the job, persuading the boss that only two men would be needed to relieve the lone rider of his lucrative responsibility.

Under normal circumstances, the payroll for the mining camp at Spearfish was sent by wagon every three months. It always had an escort of four guards.

Bribed officials at the mine had informed Diamond Jim that an extra payout had been sanctioned by head office, to ease rising tensions. Fractious miners had threatened to go on strike when a promised bonus had not been forthcoming. To appease the irate troublemakers, the company had agreed to the payout. For the purpose of cutting costs, a single rider had been dispatched along the old Indian trail.

Stoner knew that this was a heaven-sent opportunity to increase his dwindling funds. It was also Newcombe's opportunity to kill two birds with one stone. He smiled at the thought. It was a fitting proverb.

'Jack wants us to relieve a certain payroll johnny of his burdensome load.' He grinned. The outward appearance of affability was feigned. Ramone responded by grabbing the proferred olive branch.

'No hard feelings, Cimarron,' he submitted, 'about me getting hired?'

'Of course not. Charley Newcombe don't hold with bearing grudges.' He concealed the bleak cast in his hooded gaze by turning his head away.

Ramone accepted the peace offering at face value.

'How we gonna do it, then?'

Newcombe pointed a gloved hand towards a rising surge of sun-kissed orange rocks. Five minutes later he drew his mount off the narrow trail into the shelter of the boulders and dismounted.

It was the only place within miles where an effective ambush could be mounted. The trail narrowed, passing between an upsurge of weathered sandstone carved into a plethora of natural sculptures by the keening westerlies. It was no surprise, therefore, that it had been given the name of Windy Gap.

He cast a weather eye at the sun.

'The guy oughta be passing through here in about an hour.'

Newcombe then settled himself down. Rolling a smoke, he asked casually, 'Reckon you can take him out with a single shot?'

Ramone affectionately patted the barrel of his Henry carbine.

'Easy as takin' candy from a baby,' he scoffed. 'Watch and be amazed.'

His partner stifled a grin. You're the one that's gonna be surprised, turkey. But he kept the notion to himself.

Five minutes after the hour the gently even pad of shod hoofs came to their ears. The carrier was on time. And his saddle-bags looked heavy and full of greenbacks.

Hunkered down under cover, the bushwhackers waited. As they sat, tense and expectant, guns held at the ready, the squawk of a circling buzzard went unheard.

The approaching rider was still fifty yards up the trail when Coyote Bob lifted his rifle in a single fluid motion. Without seeming to take aim he pulled the trigger. The deep crack resounded off the surrounding rocks.

A red splash mushroomed across the shirt of the rider. Arms splayed wide, the impact of the lethal bullet knocked him out of the saddle. Like a rag doll he hit the ground and lay still.

Eyes glowing a firey red, facial muscles drawn tight across the angular cheekbones, Coyote emerged from cover and approached the prostrate form. He toed it once, then moved across to the skittish bay.

'Easy, boy,' he purred, catching hold of the lead rein. 'Let's have a look at what you're totin'.'

But he never got the chance to find out.

'Hey, Coyote!'

The summons from his partner made the new recruit pause and swing round on his heel. Newcombe had followed him and was standing atop a flat rock. Legs apart, a Winchester was jammed into his shoulder, the barrel pointing at Ramone's chest.

'What's your game, Charley?' he called, knowing full well that his partner had lead poisoning in mind.

'Ain't no game, mister.' Newcombe grinned. But his brutal face was oozing pure hate. The sickly smile dissolved in a feral bark as he continued: 'I lied, birdbrain. Grudges and Cimarron Charley go together like aces and eights. And maybe you don't know it, but your carcass is worth a heap of dough . . . dead or alive!' He couldn't resist a crazed chuckle.

'Guess which I cotton to. Prepare to meet your Maker, sucker!'

So it had been a set-up all along.

Ramone cursed his foolishness. He should never have trusted the hard-boiled gunslinger. Too late for regrets now.

'You dirty stinkin' rat!' he snarled. 'Ain't got the guts to call me out like a real man, face to face.'

In desperation, he levered his rifle. The weapon lifted, arcing towards the double-crossing Judas. But Newcombe was ready. Two slugs in rapid succession took Ramone out. A throaty gurgle issued from between clenched teeth as life was driven from the punctured torso. Then he joined the cash carrier in the hereafter.

An ominous silence settled over the grim execution site. It was broken by an eerie hooting from a desert owl. But Newcombe was unfazed. The killer was well pleased with the outcome of his machinations.

A look of satisfaction crossed his leering visage. Events were slotting into place just as expected. All he needed to do now was bury the payroll messenger and his effects somewhere off the trail where they would not be discovered. The guy's mount was released. It would find its own way home.

Coyote Bob's corpse was fastened to his own horse. It would serve as a reminder to the good citizens of Del Norte that Charley Newcombe was not a man to be messed with. A dependable gunhand who was pre-pared to go after undesirables and bring them in.

Dead or alive!

44

A slow smile cracked his hard expression as the artful killer surveyed the Wanted poster he had removed from his pocket. With eager relish, and not for the first time, he perused the details.

Wanted for robbery and murder: Robert Ramone, known as Coyote Bob. An outline of his crimes followed. The penned drawing of the outlaw bore little relation to reality. And here was the best bit. Reward offered: $500. A harsh laugh laced with venom spewed from Newcombe's untidy mouth. What a joke! One outlaw hunting down another.

As a potential candidate for sheriff of Del Norte, Newcombe had claimed the right to inspect the collection of Wanted dodgers gathering dust in Ben Stockley's desk drawer. This one was of fairly recent origin.

There had been no sign of anyone purporting to be a certain Blackfoot Reno. He surmised that the dodger in Ramone's possession was old, and had long since been discarded by the authorities.

In consequence it was an upbeat Cimarron Charley Newcombe who sat on a tree-stump overlooking the dreary settlement. Yessirree. *Two birds with one stone.* The mine payroll for Diamond Jim and the reward money for himself. Not a bad day's work.

But he did not want to enter Del Norte until after dark. By taking a little-used back trail, he hoped to avoid the possibility of being spotted with his macabre charge. Questions regarding the absence of Stoner's men at the time the robbery was being committed might well raise suspicions at some later date.

A blazing firmament slowly played across the western skyline in dramatic form. Shot through with streaks of purple, blue and orange, it was a sight to behold. Though not for Charley Newcombe. Jittery agitation chewed at his nerves. And it showed by the number of discarded stogie butts scattered around his feet.

Patience did not figure as one of the gunslinger's dubious talents.

At last, murky shadows of dusk began to enfold the landscape. Newcombe ground out his last smoke and mounted up.

In Del Norte, people were gathering in the Panhandle saloon. Seats had been laid out in rows. At the far end, a table was perched on the raised platform normally occupied by musicians.

The meeting had been called by Jim Stoner. Notices were posted all over town advertising the event. The idea was ostensibly to allow the various candidates for sheriff and mayor to put forward their cases.

In truth however, he intended to reveal Russ Wikeley's hidden past. He was convinced that once the good citizens of Del Norte were made aware that their prime candidate was nothing more than a bandit on the run and wanted for murder, they would turn against him. The twin likenesses were proof of his skulduggery and ignominious deception.

That would leave the door wide open for the solidly reliable denouncer of this heinous scandal to step into the shoes of town mayor. And for his own man to pin on the sheriff's badge. Diamond Jim would be a winner all round. And just to ensure that everybody supported him, his opening declaration was that *pièce de résistance* that was always a crowd-pleaser.

'Drinks are on the house!'

Stoner had allowed each candidate to speak, before rising slowly to his feet. With a serious regard, indicating a sense of duty and the burdonsome weight of responsibility, he scanned the assembled throng. No words issued from his tight-lipped mouth as he waited for total silence. All eyes focused on the last speaker of all.

Then he delivered the unequivocal condemnation.

Not in the searing tones of a fire-and-brimstone preacher, but slowly and with a measured succinctness that would be all the more powerful. Reaching into his leather document case, Stoner removed two sheets and held them up side by side facing the attentive audience.

'Perhaps Mr Wikeley would like to explain these.'

A low buzz of muttered voices broke out. Puzzled frowns passed between members of the audience. Those at the back leaned forward trying to make out what the sheets portrayed.

Stoner maintained a deadpan look as he signalled for two occupants of front-row seats to step forward.

Russ took little heed of Jim Stoner's actions. He had delivered a rousing speech and felt certain that he commanded the backing of the majority in the room. Being at the far end of the table, he could not see what Stoner had shown to the audience.

47

It was the baffled query of one observer that jerked him from a dreamy reflection of how he would run the town once elected.

'Who in tarnation is Blackfoot Reno?'

'Looks mighty like the other guy,' observed his sidekick.

'And who might that be, sir?' enquired Stoner in a flat tone that barely concealed his elation.

The pair suddenly realized what they were viewing. Startled eyes swung towards the man sitting at the end of the table.

One pointed an accusing finger.

'Damned if'n it ain't the photographer.'

'A bounty hunter arrived in town the other day to claim the reward for Blackfoot Reno,' continued Stoner, arrowing an accusive glare at his opponent. 'His name is Coyote Bob Ramone and he was all for gunning this man down in cold blood.' The speaker's voice had assumed a fervent tone that implied dedication to civic duty. 'But I persuaded Mr Ramone that in Del Norte we do things according to the rule of law.'

'What's goin' on?' hollered a grizzled miner from somewhere in the middle of the increasingly restive crowd. 'You gonna let the rest of us in on the secret?' A drone of agreement followed this demand.

Jim Stoner turned to face his adversary.

'The floor is all yours, Mr Wikeley. Or perhaps I should say. . . .' A wry smirk broke across his rugged features before he added, 'Mr Reno! Perhaps you would care to explain why a wanted murderer is running for the vital office of sheriff.'

An expectant hush descended over the gathering. Neither a cough nor a whispered aside broke the tense silence.

The object of their attention was confounded. A myriad of confused thoughts swirled around his befuggled head. So his ignominious past had at last caught up, after all this time.

The realization punched him in the guts. Only three other men knew about the ignominious history surrounding Blackfoot Reno. Two were dead. But what of the third? This Coyote Bob Ramone was clearly still alive and had dogged his trail south from Montana.

Maybe the varmint was even now sitting in this audience, leering at him. Ready to claim the reward money.

Russ was ignorant of the fact that Coyote Bob had met his end at Windy Gap.

Sucking in a deep breath, he lurched to his feet. In the time it took to gather his thoughts and survey the field of accusing eyes, the whole affair flashed through his brain.

FIVE

IN THE OPEN

The sordid business had started when the bank refused to grant an extension to the mortgage loan on the Wikeley farmstead.

Russ's pa had not even been accorded the chance to harvest the summer crop of maize. Forced to give up all he held dear, Chase Wikeley and his family had moved into the town of Bigfoot. It was located on the banks of the Flathead Lake in north-west Montana. At least this enabled Chase and his son to make a modest living as fishermen.

But when the bank took over the running of the farm and brought in hired help to harvest the crop, young Russ Wikeley saw red. Witnessing strangers reaping the profits from all their hard work was more than he could take.

A loyal and devoted friend, Russ was also an implacable enemy to those who crossed him. Disparaging

comments regarding the slump of the Wikeley circumstances had led to cracked heads and bloody noses.

Only the calming influence of his close buddy Grey
Dog Parkin had prevented lethal gunplay. Dog was a
half-breed whose father was a Blackfoot chief. His wise
counsel, however, came up against a brick wall. Russ
was determined to avenge the dishonour suffered by
his family.

'Them skunks are gonna pay dear for treating us
like this,' he railed at his tall rangy sidekick. They were
hunched over cold beers in the town's only saloon.
'That crop shoulda been ours for the selling.'

As more beer was consumed, a devious plan began
to form in the wronged nester's mind. Grey Dog tried
every form of argument to dissuade his partner from
the bleak trail on which he was set. All to no avail.

The following afternoon found the pair concealed
on the edge of the broad swath of maize. Now fully
mature, the crop rose to a height of over six feet. A
vast ocean of dull green and ochre swaying in the
gentle breeze, it effectively concealed their move-
ments from the farmhouse at the opposite side of the
field. Tinder-dry from the long hot summer, the stalks
enfolding the ripe corn cobs would require only a
slight touch to precipitate a raging inferno.

'Are you sure this is what you want, my friend?'

The 'breed's plea fell on deaf ears as the vesta
ignited.

'Here's your answer, Dog,' came back the crazed
snarl as a tallow brand burst into flames. The cheer-
lessly resolute glint was enough to silence any further

51

remonstrations. Grey Dog shrugged. He might not agree with his buddy's actions, but there was no way he would desert him.

What the fire-raisers were unaware of was that the harvest crew had arrived to begin work.

'What in tarnation is goin' on here?' a heavyset labourer blurted out on stumbling across the two avenging angels. 'You'll burn the whole goddamned crop down if you ain't careful.'

Russ quickly recovered from the unexpected intrusion. 'That's the idea.' He grinned, palming his revolver. 'And won't it make a fitting funeral pyre for that skulking land-grabber?' The gun wagged ominously at the hovering farm worker. 'Now step back and let us get on with our own work.'

'Shoot 'em down, Ramirez!'

The raucous holler to his hidden confederate saw Russ diving to one side. A bullet ploughed into the ground where he had stood seconds earlier. The torch flew out of his left hand. It landed on the nearest cluster of maize stooks which instantly caught fire.

His own revolver belched flame. A single bullet struck the second man in the chest. It was a killing shot.

'Stay where you are, mister,' snapped Dog, jabbing his own pistol at the threatening figure who had unwittingly disturbed their plans. 'You don't wanna go the same way as your friend.'

The crop quickly caught. Huge tongues of orange flame were now rapidly devouring the maize. Crackling and spitting, the conflagration was unstoppable, its destructive force inevitable.

Russ smiled. But it was tinged with regret. He had killed a man. Had such a sacrifice been worth the effort? Too late for recriminations now. The deed was done, the die cast. From this moment onward, he would become a wanted man, a felon on the run from the law.

Guilt for dragging his buddy into this turmoil resulted in a desperate plea aimed at the remaining workman.

'This guy ain't had nothing to do with all this,' he told the gang foreman. 'He was trying to stop me.' Then, turning to Grey Dog, he injected a note of forceful urgency into his voice. 'Weren't you, fella? So just throw down your gun and join this guy here.'

'Don't make me laugh, mister,' scoffed the burly foreman. 'He threatened to shoot me. So he's in this up to his neck, just like you.'

Grey Dog's thick eyebrows lifted in acceptance of the inevitable.

'Man right. We are in this to the end, partner,' he said.

'Guess you're right,' Russ replied despondently. 'Can you ever forgive me?'

Grey Dog shrugged off the apology. More urgent matters needed their attention. 'Let's just get out of here before fire brings the whole damn territory down on our necks. Once we're in the clear, then look to the future.'

Russ responded with a curt nod of assent. The half-breed had a point.

'Keep him covered while I get a rope,' he said.

In five minutes the man was securely tied to a lone cottonwood some fifty feet from the edge of the blazing inferno.

The two fugitives mounted up.

'You won't get away with this,' rasped the angry captive. 'I'll make sure they hunt you down for what you done to poor old Ramirez.'

A melancholic air settled over the reluctant killer.

'Believe me, mister, I sure do regret your buddy getting killed,' he stressed, hoping the tethered man would accept his contrition. It was genuine.

But there was no going back now.

A brittle note of bravado crept into his parting remark. 'You tell the new owner of that farm it was Reno Wixx who burnt his crop down. You remember that name: *Reno Wixx*! I'm just a sympathetic vigilante who don't cotton to thieving land-grabbers.'

He couldn't resist using the same initials, hoping that a different name would avert any suspicion that his family was involved. The last thing he wanted was their being made scapegoats for his rash behaviour.

Quickly spurring away from the burning crop, the two fugitives headed north along the broad meandering valley of the Whitefish. Only once did Russ, or Reno Wixx as he was now called, turn to survey their back trail. A column of white smoke drifted across the flats occupied by the cropland. Already much of the maize had been destroyed.

At least he had done something right, although dragging Grey Dog into his lawless scheme had not been part of the original plan. Too late to worry about that now. He cast a brief glance at the dark profile of his steadfast *compadre*. As though carved from a chunk of granite the Indian's solidly dependable features registered no disquiet.

They had been riding for upwards of two hours before Reno broke the silence.

'Where do we go from here?'

Without any hesitation, Grey Dog voiced his opinion.

'Go stay with my people on Willow Creek. Father is Spotted Tail, chief of northern Blackfoot.' Dog gave a wisely serious nod of his chiselled head. 'He will welcome you as my blood brother. Mother may be less easy to convince that our sudden appearance is inoffensive. So no mention of real reason. Our secret.' His ruddy face cracked into a half-smile as he tapped the large beaky snout.

They reached the tented encampment four days later.

It proved to be an ideal setting for the reluctant lawbreakers to hide out, at least for a spell until such time as they could make plans. Grey Dog was among his own people. He slotted into tribal life with a natural ease.

The Blackfoot had also been most welcoming to his sidekick. But Reno understood that sooner or later he would want to leave. The Indian lifestyle was not for him.

For the present, however, it offered security from arrest. Far from any white townships, the tribes had to be self-sufficient. They made full use of all that their environment had to offer. Buffalo and bear provided almost everything that was required in the way of food, clothing and tools. Nothing was wasted.

Reno enjoyed the peace and tranquility of this remote hill country. He would roam the desolate terrain making his own contribution to the tribal larder. It was whilst out on one of these expeditions that he chanced upon the opportunity to repay all the kindness he had been shown.

Rounding a rocky promontory, the trail narrowed to little more than a ledge, forcing him to dismount. Exercising infinite care, he led the horse along the precarious shelf. On the left a sheer rock wall soared upwards disappearing into the heavens. To the right lay a deep ravine.

Halfway along his sensitive hearing picked up a sound alien to the remote terrain. He stopped, listening intently.

There it was again: a human cry for help.

Somebody was in trouble.

He tethered the horse, unhooked his lariat and moved forward gingerly. Loose gravel indicated where the unknown traveller had come to grief.

'Hello down there! Can you hear me?' he called, peering over the edge into the dark void. A groan of pain was the only reply. Whoever was down there was badly injured. But at least he was still alive.

He tied the rope to a tree root and began climbing down into the black hole of the ravine. Gripping the rough hemp with both hands he leaned out and gradually abseiled down the cliff face, using the cracks and fissures to steady his descent.

At last he reached bedrock.

The injured traveller was White Owl, the ten-year-old son of Spotted Tail and brother to Grey Dog. He had been away from the camp for four days. Nobody had displayed any concern. Young Indian braves were encouraged to venture out into the wilderness alone to fend for themselves. Absences of more than a week were not uncommon.

The boy's right leg was bent at a grotesque angle. It was swollen, the bone was sticking through the bare skin. Blood dripped from numerous cuts and abrasions.

'How long have you been down here?' asked Reno. He unscrewed his water bottle and dribbled the life-giving fluid into the boy's cracked lips.

'This third day,' croaked the boy, trying desperately to conceal the pain and hurt.

Reno hid his dismay. Any longer and the boy would have died. If not from his injuries then from some wild predator.

'You're darned lucky I came along,' observed the boy's saviour while he stripped off his leather chaps. He began cutting them into long, thick straps with his knife. 'I'm gonna tie you on to my back,' he explained. 'That's the only way I can get you out of here.'

White Owl nodded his understanding. His eyes were half-closed, his breathing shallow and irregular. Delirium was setting in. The boy was done in and lucky to be alive after having experienced such a horrendous fall.

'I'm gonna lift you up to cling on to my back.' He spelt out his plan with measured deliberation so the boy understood what was happening. 'Then I'll fasten you on tight with these straps.' He took hold of the boy's shoulders firmly. 'You understand, White Owl?'

A slight jerk of the head was the boy's only indication that he had heard.

Reno tried to exercise care when raising the injured frame. The boy gritted his teeth. The movement, however carefully engineered, must have caused excrutiating agony. But the young brave maintained an unflinching silence.

Having secured the boy behind him, Reno began the long haul back up to the distant ledge and safety.

At first the task seemed quite straightforward, but the boy's weight soon began to exert a brutal toll on the rescuer's physical resources. Every muscle screamed in protest. Progress slowed to a laboured crawl.

Then it happened.

Reno's grip on the rope slackened. He slipped back almost five feet. The desperate strain to halt the slide burnt his hands. He could smell the stench of burning flesh.

'Aaaaaaagh!'

The agonized bellow was more feral than human. It sounded like the manic raving of a hell hound.

Unless he dug deep, they were both heading for the happy hunting grounds.

That was when Grey Dog's advice on how to handle pain lurched back into focus. The half-breed had undergone the infamous Sun Dance. For three days he had suffered the personal agonies associated with the rite of passage without passing out. And he had done it by adopting a process of self-empowerment. This enabled him to step outside the pain and his own body.

The mystic process had helped Reno enormously to endure the brutal ministrations of a quack dentist in Grand Rapids. Drawing on every last vestage of willpower, he now dug deep. And hung on. Blood from the lacerated skin ran down his arm in rivulets.

Slowly and methodically, he forced mind and body to work in unison. Time had no meaning. Only the steady movement of hand over hand as, like a fly on a wall, he clawed his way back up to the ledge.

The ride back to the Indian camp was easy by comparison.

In recognition of this noble deliverance, Reno Wixx became known as Blackfoot Reno. He was made an honorary member of the tribe, the highest accolade for a white man. Thereafter he proudly wore two eagle feathers in his hat and an embroidered vest specially made by the boy's mother, Jessica May Parkin.

After three months in the company of the Indians, Reno was getting itchy feet. Much as he respected and admired the tribal culture, he longed to mix with his own kind. His wish was to settle down eventually in some place where he could resume life under his proper name.

For some weeks, Grey Dog had sensed that his friend was becoming restless. So it came as no surprise when Reno's announcement that he was going to leave was at last out in the open.

'If you go, then Grey Dog follow,' asserted the Indian bluntly.

There was no uncertainty, no hesitation in the Blackfoot's resolute decision to accompany his blood brother into the unknown.

They broke camp the following morning as night was surrendering its Stygian grip. Accompanied by a feisty packmule, the two partners began the long journey east across Montana's northern plains.

The heartfelt wishes of Spotted Tail and his pale-face wife went with them. Young White Owl was particularly sad to see the white man depart. They had become very close since the traumatic events of the boy's rescue. He steadfastly refused to sanction their departure until Reno promised that some day he would return.

SIX

YELLOW HAMMER

Seven days passed before they reached the first settlement. Yellow Hammer was much like any other town that served the local ranching community. Sleepy and peaceful, it dozed in the midday sun as the two dusty riders brought their mounts to a halt beside a hitching post.

Reno nodded his approval. This seemed like a suitable place to stick around for a spell. The two buddies dismounted, slapped the trail dust from their duds and headed off up the street in search of the nearest saloon. It turned out that the Maverick was the town's only watering hole.

Spurs jingling, they stepped inside the dimly lit interior. The steady hum of voices faded as the newcomers strode across to the bar. A myriad stony eyes followed them.

'What'll it be, stranger?' asked the breezy bartender.

'Beer for me,' was Reno's perky answer. Then turning to Grey Dog he said, 'What's your poison, buddy?'

Before the barman could respond, a gruff voice interrupted.

'You're welcome to enjoy the beer, mister. But we don't serve red scum in this town.'

Reno stiffened. This place was clearly not the affable town he'd assumed it was. Even though the half-breed Blackfoot had chosen to attire himself in white man's gear, his tribal origins were unmistakable. If the ruddy features and sloping forehead did not give the game away, the knotted plait hanging down his back certainly did.

Ignoring the menace spilling from the blunt insinuation, Reno snapped out, 'We'll both have beers. And make them large and cold. Our throats are dry as sandpaper.'

The trembling bartender hovered uncertainly. He was well aware of the town's attitude to Indians. Recent attacks by Sioux raiding parties had tarred all Indian tribes with the same brush. But as a business-man, he always tried to avoid taking sides unless personally threatened.

'Are you deaf or just plain stupid?' came the brittle response from behind the newcomers when the speaker found that his threat was being ignored. 'This town don't cotton to redskins.' Chairs scraped back as numerous onlookers decided that trouble was brewing. They had no desire to be in the firing line if gunplay erupted.

'It OK, Reno,' Grey Dog urged while trying to pull his friend towards the door. 'Not thirsty any more.'

But Reno's taut features were set like concrete. He shrugged off the calming gesture.

'Pour the beer, mister! And make it quick!'

Reno's waspish retort sliced through the tense atmosphere like a knife through butter. Beer splashed into a glass. Most of it spilled down the sides of the glass as the frightened barman pushed the glasses across the bar top before retreating to the far end.

Reflected in the rear mirror, Reno could easily discern the source of the threats. A brawny tough clad in range garb and sporting a straggly ginger beard was flanked by two other mean-eyed critters. Their hands were poised above holstered revolvers.

Reno's brittle reaction to the blunt intimidation elicited a churlish snarl from the big man. He stepped forward, his left hand grabbing at Reno's shoulder with the intention of spinning him around.

It succeeded. But not in the manner intended.

The heavy beer glass swung in a wide arc and cracked hard against the side of the bully's face. Red Butler staggered under the impact. Blood poured from his lacerated cheek.

One of Butler's sidekicks stepped forward growling 'Damned Injun lover!' as he attempted an underarm lunge at the white man's guts with a Bowie knife. Grey Dog's arm slammed down, his rigid hand snapping the attacker's forearm. It was a clean break.

The man screamed as he lurched back hugging his smashed limb. The knife spun away and clattered against a spittoon.

'Much obliged, Dog,' smiled an appreciative Reno Wixx. His keen gaze stayed fixed on the continuing threat posed by the remaining assailants.

Red Butler was no milksop. A formidable grappler, well-versed in the brutal art of bar-room brawling, he quickly shook off the stunning effects of the assault. But this was no occasion for fisticuffs. Stepping back a pace, he grabbed for his revolver.

Before it had even cleared leather a bullet from Reno's own gun drilled into the rising hogleg. It smashed the mechanism, gunmetal scoring deep furrows in the bully's hand. Butler stumbled against a table, his face twisted in pain.

In the blink of an eye Reno had swung his palmed revolver to cover the last of the trio.

'Well, mister, you got any ambitions to be a hero?' Reno smirked, holding the stupefied gape of the remaining attacker. With assured conviction he eased off the Colt's hammer, spun it on his middle finger before expertly flipping the gun back into its holster.

Both thumbs hooked into the front of the gunbelt as he stood facing the man. The jasper's mouth hung open in shock. All previous bravado had evaporated. The tables had been turned in no uncertain terms.

Chester Ludd was no hero. Just a simple cowpoke, not some mean-eyed gunslinger like this guy. Both hands shot up, reaching for the tobacco-stained ceiling.

'Don't shoot, mister,' he whined. 'I've had enough.'

'Then get these turkeys out of here, pronto,' ordered Reno with a brisk jerk of his head. 'Looks to me like they need the attentions of a medic.'

'S-sure thing,' concurred Ludd, helping his confederates out of the saloon.

After the sorry trio had left the Maverick, the Indian declared with a wide grin: 'And now perhaps we can be allowed to enjoy our beer in peace. What you say to that, Reno?'

'I say you've hit the nail on the head,' agreed his partner, adding with a wry smirk: 'Or should I say beer glass.' Hoots of laughter accompanied the astute witticism. He signalled for fresh glasses. 'And maybe this kind bartender will be willing to forgo payment on account of all the trouble his customers have caused.'

The beer-puller was more than eager to please.

While the two buddies were enjoying their drink, two sinister-looking jiggers in the corner were giving them a more than cursory once-over.

Their hooded eyes kept flicking from a sheet of paper they were studying to the two drinkers leaning on the bar.

'Has to be them,' hissed Coyote Bob, slurping at the bottle of redeye they were sharing. 'The whitey's name is Reno and his buddy has to be Grey Dog.'

The man sitting beside him was some ten years older. He had the same shifty look, the same thin lips and hooked nose. But Deke Ramone had an altogether more commanding assurance. It showed in his tailor-made duds; the sharp blue suit with knife-edged creases in the trousers, a crisp white shirt and bootlace necktie. A born gambler, he continued with his game of solitaire.

The younger Ramone read out the charge.

'Wanted for murder and criminal damage to property.' Coyote Bob twisted his lip. 'Five hundred bucks plus three for the 'breed don't seem much to me.'

Deke gave his brother a pitying look. His manicured fingers slid across the all-important legend above the pen drawings of the wanted felons.

Dead or alive!

'Eight hundred will give us a grubstake to make our fortunes on that new gold strike down in the Black Hills country,' he said, raising a languid eye towards the unsuspecting pair at the bar. 'And this is how we play it.'

Deke Ramone then went on to outline his plan.

Half an hour later Blackfoot Reno and his sidekick left the dubious pleasures of the Maverick saloon. They stepped down into the dusty street and headed back towards their tethered mounts.

Grey Dog didn't stand a chance.

One second he was joshing his partner, the next his arms were flung skyward as two 44.40 bullets ploughed into his back. He crashed to the ground, his life snuffed out in an instant. The Great Spirit had called Grey Dog earlier than expected.

No warning had been issued. It was the work of a backshooter, the most craven of all killers. Reno bent low, throwing himself behind a water trough. Two more shots rang out, chewing lumps of street dirt from the spot he had just vacated. He ducked low, revolver palmed and ready.

The bushwhaker must have been waiting for them to leave the saloon. Was it a fourth member of the troublemakers' group that he had missed? Or maybe the name of Reno Wixx had spread this far east and these were bounty hunters. He tended towards this latter assumption. But this was no time for idle speculation. He was in a pickle, not knowing how many there were.

A flickering black silhouette impinged itself on his probing gaze as he quickly scanned the rooftops on the far side of the street. The gunman was trying to reposition himself for a better shot. Reno waited. He had no choice, being trapped behind the water butt.

'Drop your hardware, Blackfoot,' said a brittle yet firm voice to his rear. 'One false move and you get the same as your Indian buddy.'

Reno cursed himself for being caught unawares.

'You a bounty killer?' he asked calmly.

'One and the same,' came back the stony reply. 'And just remember you're worth just as much dead as alive.'

'And how much is that?'

Deke Ramone hawked out a lurid guffaw.

'Not much,' he jeered. 'Only five hundred. But it's enough to give me and my brother a grubstake.'

So there was one other bushwhacker around. He must be the one on the roof who had taken out poor old Grey Dog. The thought precipitated a charge of hatred down his spine. No way was he surrendering to skunks like these.

He was still gripping his revolver. And it was hidden from view. Sucking in a deep breath, he rapidly figured out his next move. It might be his last. But that was a chance he was prepared to take.

'OK, mister, you've got the drop on me.'

Reno's head dropped, shoulders sagging in apparent dejection at being outdrawn. He sensed the release of tension in the guy's audible sigh of relief. It was now or never. Left shoulder spinning he brought the concealed revolver around in a scything arc.

Cock and fire! Again. Cock and fire!

Deke Ramone was caught wrongfooted. Clutching at his shattered chest with one hand, he desperately attempted to squeeze the trigger. A third blast from Reno's six-gun and the bounty hunter pitched backwards.

The splayed-out corpse evoked a howl of anguish from across the street. The chilling wail floated across the killing ground.

'Nooooooo!'

Coyote Bob lurched from behind the cover of a false-front gable on seeing his brother bite the dust. Reno felt the sting of lead creasing his cheek as the younger Ramone let fly. But his aim was erratic, the calm deliberation needed for a killing shot had crumbled.

Head tucked away beneath the lip of the horse trough, Reno quickly thumbed fresh shells into his revolver. The range was too long for the effective use of a handgun. So he aimed high, pumping off three shots in rapid succession.

At least one struck home. A cry of pain produced a grim smile as Bob Ramone's rifle clattered down into the street below. The bushwhacker dropped out of sight, giving Reno the opportunity to sprint down the street and leap into the saddle. Hugging the neck of his cayuse, the fugitive kicked out of Yellow Hammer at a frenetic pace.

SEVEN

UNEXPECTED OUTCOME

'Well Mr . . . Wikeley?' The sanctimonious tone of the speaker jarred Russ back to the present. 'We're all eager to hear what you have to say.' Jim Stoner aimed a leery smirk at the ashen-faced figure to his left.

'Come on, Wikeley, or whatever you call yourself,' shouted an unidentifiable voice from the audience. 'Explain yourself!'

'And it better be good,' crowed another voice.

A murmur of agreement rippled through the assembly.

Russ surveyed the restive throng with some trepidation. One face stood out from the rest. Eleanor sat motionless in the second row. She was accompanied by her mother and Doc Harding. Dismay, shock and a host of similar emotions registered on her stricken countenance.

Worst of all for Russ was the expression depicting shame and disgrace at the notion of being associated with a wanted felon.

How could he explain himself? How could he justify his appointment as a law officer when all he amounted to was a ne'er-do-well with a price on his head?

The pleading regard that it was all a huge error, a case of mistaken identity brought a tear to his eye. This was no misunderstanding. Blackfoot Reno was all they said he was, and more.

But hadn't he been driven to it by that grasping turd of a land-grabber in Bigfoot? And the shooting of the harvest worker really had been a mistake. He hadn't meant to kill the guy, just slow him up some. Then there was the bounty hunter. Well, those critters were no better than the poor galoots they were hunting. He had been a model citizen since his arrival in Del Norte. He'd always paid his dues on time, supported the church and local good works.

These thoughts convinced Russ that he had a solid case.

Squaring his shoulders, and with a renewed confidence that right was on his side, Russ silenced the expectant gathering with a raised hand and a determined stare.

'Can anybody here deny that I haven't put a foot wrong since arriving here two years since?' he began, punching out every syllable with vigour and a challenging regard. He paused to allow the impact of his cogent delivery to sink in. 'And before today, would any here present have considered that Russ Wikeley

71

could stoop so low as to become a cold-hearted killer?'

Nobody disputed that supposition.

'Sure,' he conceded, nodding sagely. 'I've made mistakes. And I did kill a man. But it was only to save my own hide after he shot at me first.'

And so the address continued. It was a heart-felt and passionate plea for understanding. When Russ eventually sat down it was to a round of applause. Muted perhaps, but the previous open hostility had evaporated. Jim Stoner was looking worried.

That was when Dewlap Jenson chose to put the icing on the cake by reminding everybody how Russ Wikeley had single-handedly stymied a bank robbery. Following the delivery of this solid reminder, the newspaperman leapt to his feet. Sagging jowls quivered with an ardent zeal as he addressed the assembly.

'You all know me,' he began. 'Hasn't the *Tribune* always printed the goddamned truth? Pardon my French, ladies,' he hastened to placate Betsy Harding and her daughter. 'Brought you the latest news as it stands with no frills and no prejudice?'

Various nods of agreement greeted the contention as he continued, 'I've known this man since he first arrived in Del Norte. A more honest and upright citizen I have yet to meet. I ain't much on socializing. Newsmen have to remain neutral, unbiased. But I tell you folks that I count this man as my best buddy. And if that don't prove he's no brigand,' he concluded emphatically, 'then I'm a lop-eared mule.'

'Make that a turkey, Dewlap, and you're right!' chuckled an old miner.

'Ain't paid much attention to them wiggly ears before,' added another wit.

But Dewlap's assertive backing had turned the tide. The blithe comments elicited a cacophany of good-natured laughter that rapidly spread around the room. Folks were on their feet, all eager to shake the hand of their prospective sheriff. Even young Brad Craven gave his support, saying he was withdrawing from the race and would back Russ's campaign all the way.

But all Russ was bothered about was the reaction of Eleanor Harding to his heart-felt apology. It had drained him. A drink was badly needed to calm jaded nerves. Nonetheless, he was on tenterhooks as she approached the stage. Her radiant smile was all he wanted to see. The back-slapping and assurances of support went unheeded.

Only Jim Stoner had a glum face. His ploy to dis-credit the popular photographer had backfired. A grimace of pure hate stabbed the retreating back of the winner. Unless a miracle occurred Stoner was fin-ished in Del Norte.

Unbeknown to Diamond Jim, that much-needed phenomenon had just arrived at the rear of the Panhandle saloon in the form of a deceased Coyote Bob Ramone.

Cimarron Charley was waiting in the upstairs office when Stoner returned. He had left Bob Ramone's corpse in the storeroom below.

'How'd it go?' was Stoner's brisk enquiry.

'Easy as pie,' answered the bodyguard. 'And there

was more dough than we figured.' He lifted the bulging saddle-bags as if they were ton weights. 'More than enough to grease a few palms and get us both elected.'

The smile of seconds before vanished and a despondent glower once again settled over Stoner's pasty features.

'It's gonna take more than a few measly dollars to sort this mess out,' he grumbled, splashing a heavy measure of Scotch into a glass and sinking it in a single gulp. The fiery liquor appeared to have no effect. Another measure followed in quick succession. Seeing his empire about to crumble about his ears was not a happy notion.

'What yuh gettin' at, boss?' posed the bewildered killer.

The whole sorry business of the election meeting was blurted out amid a series of growled imprecations. Being made to feel smaller than a church mouse was difficult to swallow.

'And there struts the bastard who's the cause of it all.'

Newcombe followed Stoner's baleful gaze across the street. The bodyguard scowled. He could see his own future also disappearing down the plughole.

'Where's Ramone?' Stoner had just noticed the absence of the new gunman.

'He didn't make it,' replied Newcombe, concealing a satisfied leer. He was top dog again. 'Stray bullet took him out.'

Then an idea began to form in his devious mind.

It was the perfect answer to their dilemma, a simple yet foolproof scheme. One that would indubitably scupper their adversary once and for all. That would then leave the race wide open, with no effective opposition. Indeed Stoner Enterprises would be hailed as the only genuine force for law and order in the town.

Stoner was at first unconvinced. Gloomy ruminations had dulled his brain cells. It was the bodyguard's persistence that eventually coaxed a new fire into being. The crackling flame of revenge quickly stoked up to a raging inferno that burnt deep into Stoner's feckless heart. The steely glint and tight jawline indicated a fierce and implacable resolve to rid himself of this tiresome annoyance.

Cimarron had posed the initial idea. Now, it was a rejuvenated Jim Stoner who set about fine-tuning the details of its implementation.

Russ was taking a well-deserved breather. It had been an exhausting day. He considered himself fortunate to have emerged unscathed. Jim Stoner's endeavour to pour discredit and shame on to his campaign had left him in a stronger position than he could ever have anticipated. Even Eleanor seemed to look on him in a different light. It was all rather bizarre.

Suddenly the door of his studio opened and a young urchin breezed in.

'Got a message for you, Mr Wikeley,' he declared, holding out a folded sheet of paper.

The photographer frowned. Who could be sending him messages at this late hour? Accepting the missive, he dug into his pocket and hooked out a quarter which he flipped into the air. The boy snatched it with dexterity like a lizard catching a fly. He bit down on the coin before departing.

As Russ opened up the letter his eyes widened in surprise. It was signed by Jim Stoner. This was proving more unexpected by the minute. The message was brief and appeared to be offering an olive branch.

Dear Russ

I can't say that I was not disappointed when you got the town behind you at the election meeting. But Jim Stoner is nothing if not generous in defeat. I know when to cut my losses so intend selling up and leaving Del Norte soon as things can be arranged. No grudges or malice on my part. And to show there are no hard feelings, how about coming over to my place now for a drink so's we can shake on it. Come up the back stairs. No sense in my regulars thinking that the boss has gone all soft.

(signed) Diamond Jim Stoner.

After reading through the message a second time, Russ scratched his head. He was undecided what to make of this unexpected show of contrition on the part of the tricky operator.

If he was indeed ready to throw in the towel, Russ Wikeley certainly wouldn't stand in his way, nor harbour any malicious rancour. It was a touch on the late side. But what the heck! A drink with a remorseful adversary would finish the day on a positive note.

After locking up he crossed the street and headed

down a narrow passage to approach the Panhandle from the rear. A dog growled somewhere away to his left. It was followed by a cat screeching in terror. Conflict is never far away in a gold-mining town.

Beyond the glare of the main street the gloom of pervading darkness was all the more oppressive. His pace slowed as he carefully picked a course through the abandoned detritus that always accumulated in back alleys. The Panhandle was the largest building on the west side of Alder Street, its elongated spread pushing back from adjacent structures.

A single oil lamp illuminated the back stairs which led up to the first floor where Stoner had his quarters. This was Russ's first visit, and no doubt his last. He had no wish to prolong the unexpected encounter, which in anticipation was somewhat unsettling. He couldn't dispel the view that all was not as it seemed. It was out of character, not the sort of behaviour he would ever have expected from Jim Stoner.

Anger, resentment, hatred. Yes! But a peace offering?

Maybe he should just turn around and forget all about it. But he was here now, halfway up the back stairs. He shrugged and pushed open the door at the top. It led into a dimly lit corridor.

The first door on the left was open. He was expected. A beam of light played across the linoleum floor of the corridor.

'Come in, Russ,' called out a jovial voice he recognized as belonging to the saloon owner. 'Drinks are on the table.'

Gingerly he entered the room.

Stoner was behind the large mahogany desk, a drink in one hand, cigar in the other. The greasy smile looked like it had been pasted on to the effulgent visage.

'Meet the guy who was meant to have upset your little game of playing happy families.' The smile had hardened, the black look was cold as a mountain stream. 'But better late than never. Pity you had to come in here and shoot him down. Then rob my safe.'

Laid out on the floor with two bullet holes in his chest was a man Russ didn't recognize.

His puzzled expression drew a sharp reminder.

'Remember Yellow Hammer and a gunfight on the main street?'

Once again the whole bizarre turn of events flooded back into sharp focus.

'This is, or was, Coyote Bob Ramone. You shot and killed his brother, not to mention putting Bob here out of action for a couple of months. The poor sucker came here intent on revenge.' A gurgled chortle lurched from Stoner's grinning maw. 'And he's suc-ceeded. Just not in the manner he figured.'

Russ's eyes widened.

A set up!

It was all a devilish plan to double-cross him. And he'd walked right in and allowed it to happen. What a greenhorn!

'Why you dirty, rotten—'

His hand dropped to the holstered revolver he always toted as a matter of course. But his sudden grasp of the dire situation came too late.

Even as he realized the gravity of the predicament into which he had blundered, Cimarron Charley emerged from the behind the door and clubbed him over the back of the head with the butt end of a .45.

Blackness engulfed his stunned brain. Russ crumpled as a second blow sealed his fate. The last thing he recalled before the lights went out were the grotesque guffaws pursuing him down the dark tunnel.

The two villains had planned their subterfuge well.

In silence they set about ensuring that Russ Wikeley would be arrested for murder and robbery. Newcombe fired two bullets from Russ's revolver into a cushion. The blast was muffled by the flock stuffing. Then he positioned the gun in the victim's hand, his finger around the trigger. Pig's blood obtained from the kitchen was dribbled over the dead man's wounds making it appear that the killing had only just occurred.

In the meantime, Stoner had opened up the safe and grabbed a wad of greenbacks. He stuffed them into the unconscious man's pockets.

'Have we missed anything?' he said, standing back, shifty eyes flitting every which way. 'This ruse has got to be convincing. Stockley might be an old has-been, but he ain't no half-wit.'

Now the moment of having to satisfy the existing lawdog of the validity of their deception had arrived, Charley Newcombe was a touch edgy. His nose itched. His left eyelid was twitching vigorously. A dead give away to an astute lawman.

'Pull yourself together,' rasped Stoner urgently. 'This ain't no time for getting chicken-livered. Just think of those two bounties you'll be collecting. A cool grand ain't to be sniffed at.'

That thought rallied the simpering killer. He shook off the alarm of moments before. Newcombe nodded his concurrence with the contrived scenario.

'OK, we're agreed then,' Stoner concluded. He adjusted his necktie before checking his appearance in the mirror. 'I'll go down to the bar and get the band to play some rousing tunes. A round of drinks on the house will soon have the drunken turkeys warbling. That will explain away the fact that nobody heard any gunfire.'

'And I'll wait a half-hour before luckily arriving just at the right moment to catch this critter robbing the safe.' Newcombe toed the unconscious form while adopting an appropriately sombre expression. 'He must have shot Coyote for digging up his lurid past just as the poor guy was banking some of the takings. Some guys just ain't the forgiving kind.'

'And don't forget to make it sound convincing when you blurt out the sordid discovery,' propounded Stoner. 'We can't afford no mistakes.'

'I could persuade Old Nick himself to attend a Sunday service if'n the price was right.'

Stoner's lips drew back in a lurid grin.

'Revenge and robbery.' He smirked and lit up a long thin cigar. 'The varmint will get at least a twenty stretch in the can.'

'Just where he belongs,' agreed Newcombe squaring his shoulders. 'That shiny tin star will look mighty swell pinned on a new suit. Things are looking up, boss.'

'They sure are,' agreed Diamond Jim as he handed over one of his prized Havanas to his subordinate.

EIGHT

OPEN AND SHUT

Some half an hour later, Newcombe paused at the head of the stairs leading down into the well of the saloon. He was hidden from view by a thick velvet drape. It was just after midnight and still the Panhandle was doing a roaring trade. Prospectors and cowhands mingled in a swaying throng intent on making merry.

He cast a furtive peeper down into the maelstrom of activity.

In a booth at the far end, Diamond Jim was in serious negotiations with some miners regarding an exchange of gold dust. Newcombe gave the conflab a sly grin. Judging by the slumped shoulders, the boss as always had got the better of the deal. It was a case of take it or leave it. The nearest assay office to Del Norte was at Deadwood, where even less favourable terms applied.

Curt nods followed and the deal was struck. Stoner pocketed a small poke in exchange for greenbacks, most of which would likely find themselves back into his pocket by the end of the night.

Once the miners had departed, Newcombe caught the boss's eye. A brief nod, a sharp intake of breath, and he was scurrying down the stairs hollering on top note.

Beads of sweat bubbled on the jittery bodyguard's forehead. His face took on a waxy pallor as Cimarron Charley Newcombe effortlessly fell into the part of a distraught employee.

'The safe's been robbed,' he shouted above the hullabaloo, 'and one of our boys has been shot down.'

Those nearest who had heard the jolting announcement stood aside to give Newcombe some space.

'I didn't hear no shots,' observed a nearby drinker.

'That's cos of all the racket from that goldarned band,' replied his partner. The Blacktails continued performing until the saloon owner silenced them with a pistol shot aimed at the floor.

'What's this all about?' piped up Diamond Jim, elbowing a passage through the rapidly quieting tumult. He laid an arm across Newcombe's shoulder apparently to calm the gunman down. 'Take it easy, Cimarron,' he soothed, 'and just tell us what happened.'

Newcombe quickly went through the charade the iniquitous pair had hatched. When he'd finished the boss asked the vital question now on everyone's lips.

'And who's the skunk that did this foul deed?'

83

Newcombe held his reply in check to increase the tension.

'It was that blamed photographer, Russ Wikeley,' announced Newcombe for all to hear. 'I caught him red-handed in the act of robbing the safe.' Then with a credible infusion of grief added, 'Pity I was too late to save Coyote.'

A stunned silence settled over the room. But only for an instant. Then all hell broke loose.

'Somebody get the sheriff,' yelled Stoner above the cacophany as he hurried up the stairs with Newcombe.

A dozen morbid voyeurs followed hot on his heels. Only the chosen few were normally given access to the upper floor. But Diamond Jim was keen to allow some of the rabble into the inner sanctum to strengthen his hand. That way, wholesale anger at the photographer's vengeful action would spread round the town like wildfire.

Five minutes later Stockley arrived and began ushering the onlookers away.

'Go get Doc Harding,' he ordered, bending over Ramone's blood-stained corpse. 'This fella looks dead all right, but we need a medic to confirm it.' His gimlet eyes then shifted to the groaning body of Russ Wikeley. 'Looks like I'm gonna have me a murder case to retire on after all.'

Russ was too stunned to protest. His head throbbed. It felt like a stampeding herd of longhorns had trampled him underfoot. With blatant disregard for legal procedure, he was hustled roughly to his feet and cuffed.

Half a dozen fists pummelled him on the way down the stairs and through the heaving mêlée. The situation was volatile. A powder keg set to blow.

Lynch law was in the air.

Not because a little-known hardcase had been killed, or that Stoner had nearly been robbed. What irked the mob most of all was that their prospective new sheriff was the perpetrator. The miners in particular felt that they had been duped, hoodwinked by false words and empty promises.

The feeling of resentment, fuelled by a copious supply of hard liquor, quickly spread. Passers-by on the sidewalk stuck their heads in the door to see what all the ruckus was about and quickly got caught up in the excitement.

Stoner and Newcombe stood to one side, content to enjoy the action.

Things could not be going better. All it needed was for some over-zealous lunkhead to decide that an ageing lawman and his greenhorn deputy were no match for a heap of tough diggers.

Then it happened.

'Let me at the bastard,' snarled one heavyweight, lunging at the prisoner with a broken bottle.

But Deputy Craven was no easy touch. It was only the young officer's swift and decisive intervention that prevented serious injury.

Crack!

The harsh blast of a Colt Peacemaker took the end of the bruiser's middle finger off at the knuckle. Twin six-guns were palmed and threatening dire consequences for anyone else who sought to take the law into their own hands as Brad Craven glowered at the stunned faces.

'Next one who tries anything like that will be joining this turkey in the slammer,' he rapped. A granite stare scanned the heaving mass of humanity.

'And there'll be no vigilante law in this town while I'm still sheriff,' added Stockley with equal vehemence. 'Now back off and give us some room.'

Like the tale of Moses and the Red Sea, the seething mass of humanity instantly parted. There was nothing like spilled blood to cool the anger of the foolhardy.

'And get this jasper to the doctor,' added the sheriff, nodding towards the bleating miner.

Once out on the street they hurriedly trundled the dazed prisoner over to the jailhouse. The sooner he was under lock and key the safer for all concerned, not least themselves. The last thing Stockley needed at this late stage in his career was to be shot down by a baying mob of vigilantes.

It was going to be a tense week before the circuit judge arrived.

On the day of the trial the town was buzzing.

Everybody within a day's ride, it seemed, had come to Del Norte. Just like Independence Day, a trial always attracted a host of snoopers, busybodies and the plain curious. Saloons and diners were thriving.

The only person not enjoying the festivities was Russ Wikeley.

Following his arrest, Eleanor Harding had broken off any further contact with the prisoner. Like all the other citizens, she had accepted his impassioned plea for clemency and understanding when the strange circumstances of his past had been revealed.

But this was a step too far. She went along with the general view that a leopard cannot change its spots.

Even Dewlap Jenson was finding it hard to reconcile the man he thought he knew with the unrebuttable evidence now stacked up against his old buddy. Even so he still maintained a neutral stance when it came to reporting the weird train of events.

'You have to believe me,' Russ urged his friend from the confines of his cell. 'I've been framed. Stoner lured me over to his place then slugged me and planted the dough.'

'Then how do you explain that guy Ramone being found shot by your gun?' enquired the perplexed editor. 'I want to believe you, Russ. But the evidence is overwhelming.' His arms were raised in impotent sorrow. 'I'm sorry, buddy, but unless a miracle happens, you're going down for a hefty spell.'

Russ bowed his head. Deep furrows of anguish creased his forehead. He slumped on to the bunk, tears of frustration tracing a path through the stubble of his ashen face.

'Even Ellie has abandoned me.' The words were flat and lifeless. Outside, the mournful howl of a cat echoed across the sun-baked landscape. A whining dog joined in the impromptu dirge.

Jenson left the jail feeling powerless.

Lying on his bunk, Russ Wikeley stared blankly at the ceiling. His eyes were glassy and lacklustre. He had surrendered all hope of the celebrated American justice coming to his aid.

It was an open-and-shut case.

On the day of the trial, the courtroom was packed to the rafters. His Honour Judge Markus Sammels was presiding. Those not able to get a seat, hovered outside, constantly probing for titbits of juicy gossip. Following the due process of law, the trial was straight-forward and quickly concluded.

After only half an hour of deliberation the jury filed back into the courtroom.

'Foreman of the jury,' Judge Sammels began in a suitably dolorous tone. 'Have you reached a verdict that you are all agreed upon?'

'We have, your honour.'

'Prisoner will stand and face the jury.'

Silence, total and heavy descended over the sombre gathering.

Then it was announced.

No surprise was apparent when the twelve good men and true delivered their unanimous verdict.

Guilty!

The judge turned to address the prisoner.

'Russell Wikeley, otherwise known as Reno Wixx or Blackfoot Reno, you have been found guilty of murder and armed robbery by a jury of your peers. Have you anything to say before sentence is passed?'

Russ appeared not to have heard. He just stared ahead. No words of his could do any good now.

'Only the positive testimony of Mr Jenson, the proprietor of the *Del Norte Tribune*, has prevented me passing the ultimate sentence. It is fortunate indeed for you that such an influential citizen was prepared to go against public opinion in support of a proven blackguard.' The judge paused, riffling papers before announcing his decision. 'You will serve twenty years of hard labour at the state penitentary.'

Once the sentence had been passed, a babble of discordant whoops and jeers broke out. Some thought it a harsh judgment, others that Sammels had deprived them of a necktie party.

Diamond Jim Stoner balked at a custodial having been granted. And he was not about to forget who was the prime cause of Wikeley having escaped the hangman's ministrations.

Dewlap Jenson had made a bitter enemy.

NINE

IN THE PEN

It was a further week before the prison wagon caught up with Judge Sammels and his sentences. Three other crestfallen captives were chained to the central locking post when Russ Wikeley joined them. From Del Norte in the Black Hills it was a gruelling trek east to the penitentiary on the north bank of the wide Missouri.

There was little attempt at conversation.

Each man brooded over the circumstances that had landed him in his current predicament. The Dakota pen was no soft option. It was rumoured to be even worse than the notorious Arizona hellhole at Yuma. And the four guards escorting the crestfallen group of convicts were quick to promote its infamous reputation.

'Watch out for the chief warder,' said one guard with a smirk. 'He ain't called the Mad Bull for nothing.'

'Get on the wrong side of that jigger and you'll end up in the kennel,' added another. He didn't enlighten the ashen-faced cons as to the nature surrounding this baleful means of correction. Raised eyebrows received a mocking chuckle. 'You'll find out soon enough.'

Day followed night with momontonous regularity as the miles to their new home were slowly eaten away. At last, on the fifth day, the bleak ochre walls of the infamous institution hove into view.

It was indeed a grimly cheerless sight.

Standing apart from the military fort and its burgeoning township, the prison's high walls towered over the small wagon as it drew to a halt outside the great oak-and-steel gate. At either end of this front wall watch-towers provided cover from the blazing sun for the ever-vigilant guards.

Peering up through red-rimmed eyes gritty with dust, Russ counted five mean-looking critters clutching rifles. They were glowering at the new intake as if they were fresh lambs to the slaughter. From this moment until he was delivered from injustice, he determined that Russ Wikeley was dead.

Arise, Blackfoot Reno!

'The Hotel Missouri,' piped up one wag of a guard. 'Make yourselves at home, boys. Cos you ain't going no place else for the foreseeable future.'

With that valedictory comment, the transit guards handed over their weary charges to the prison officials.

Processing took around an hour and included a lecture delivered in a flat monotone by the governor.

They were issued with the regulation striped prison overshirt but were allowed to retain their own trousers and boots. In addition to a tin mug and plate, they received one smelly blanket and a pillow.

One guy sniffed the air in disgust.

Instantly, the guy was struck about the head and shoulders with a heavy truncheon and the items confiscated. He fell to the floor streaming blood.

'Not to your liking, sir?' snorted the guard in a mocking tone. 'We'll see how you get on without them for a week in solitary.'

'What about a knife and fork?' enquired another prisoner imbuing the query with a sufficiently downtrodden whine to prevent more physical abuse.

'If'n you think we'd trust scum like you with deadly weapons,' scoffed a heavy-set guard, his scowling face inches from the convict, 'then you're just as stupid as you look.' Chortling at the poor guy's puzzled expression he said, 'Use your fingers like the animal you are.'

And with that crowning insult the new convicts were unceremoniously kicked all the way down the steps and into the prison courtyard. Its confined nature ensured that the temperature was always hot enough to melt the eyes of a gopher.

There they were met by the chief warder. Bull Raistrick gave each of them a welcoming jab with his heavy metal-tipped club as they passed.

In the centre of the yard was a large hole measuring ten feet square by four deep, making it impossible to stand upright. It was covered by strip steel bars with a locked opening at one side. There was no cover from the blazing sun that beat down relentlessly throughout the day. Only after the sun had shifted over the high walls was there any relief for the inmates.

Reno peered down as he passed. Only one person was incarcerated. He was crouched in a corner desperately trying to shield his head. A low groan filtered through the bars. It sounded like the keening of an animal in pain.

'Water!' a voice croaked. 'For pity's sake, give me water.'

Bull Raistrick emitted a brutal guffaw. Then he unhooked the water bottle from his belt, and poured the contents on to the floor in the pit. Before the wretched incumbent had a chance to reach out for the precious liquid, it had disappeared, soaking into the hot sandy floor.

The prisoners gasped in sympathetic accord.

This must be the infamous kennel!

'You know the rules, Jackdaw,' growled the guard aiming a glob of spital at the miserable convict. 'Water at first light and sunset only.'

With that, the shambling file carried on to the far side where the main cell blocks were located.

Entry to these was through a massive iron gate secured by a two heavy padlocks. The cells lined each side of a long corridor. Each one housed two convicts and had a sturdy oak door with a small barred aperture through which food was passed. The only furniture was a double bunk and latrine bucket. This was emptied once a day prior to the arrival of what laughingly passed for breakfast.

'Halt!'

The brusque command brought the fettered line to a shuffling standstill.

'This is gonna be your home for the duration, Reno,' snapped Raistrick, selecting a key from the large bunch hanging from his belt. The iron-studded door creaked open on rusted hinges. 'I trust you will enjoy your stay with us,' mocked the leering custodian.

There was no response to the sardonic comment. The prisoner's thoughts were elsewhere. This drew an ugly scowl from the chief warden.

'Inside,' he rasped, gesturing with a flick of his cudgel. As Reno made to enter the tiny cell, he was assisted on his way by a heavy boot which sent him sprawling on to the hard-packed earth floor. Unable to avoid the latrine bucket, its fetid contents spewed forth aggravating the already rancid odour of stale urine.

The cell door slammed shut.

'What in tarnation did yuh do that fer?' asked a peeved voice emanating from the top bunk. 'Gets bad enough in this pigsty without some clumsy galoot makin' things worse.'

A honk of muted laughter came from the outside corridor as the convict line moved on.

Red-rimmed watery eyes peered at the newcomer from a face gnarled and pitted like an ancient redwood. Lank greasy hair merged with a stringy beard, a thin red line indicating where the mouth ought to be. It barely moved as the old guy stuck a finger downwards.

'New guys allus take the lower bunk. Got any objections?'

Reno shrugged. Scrambling to his feet, he cast a jaundiced eye around the squalid quarters.

'Nice, ain't it?' cackled the old reprobate. 'You soon get used to it. Feels just like home after the first five years.' Another hearty guffaw. 'Got any snout?'

'Eh?' grunted Reno.

'Tobacco, man. It's like gold-dust in here.'

Russ delved into his pocket and pulled out the makings. He tossed it across to the old convict who immediately built himself a generous quirley. Slumping back on the grubby palliasse, he was soon lost in the euphoric bliss of his first smoke for a week. Grunts of ecstatic pleasure emerged from the grey tangle as he handed the sack of Bull Durham back.

'Keep it,' said Russ flopping on to the bottom bunk. 'You appear to have the need more than me.'

'Gee, thanks, mister,' croaked the old buzzard. 'I go under the handle of the Sagebrush Kid.'

Russ couldn't help smiling as he introduced himself. The guy looked at least sixty.

'Rus—' The prisoner caught himself just in time. 'Blackfoot Reno Wixx,' he replied, shaking the old guy's hand.

It turned out that Sagebrush had been in the pen for ten years and was due for release in three months, if he kept his nose clean. When asked about his crime, he was more than willing to explain the circumstances.

'Caught my wife in bed with the doctor,' he sniffed, puffing hard on the quirley. 'Talk about a good bedside manner. The rat was givin' her a sight more'n medication.' The old guy laughed at his own humour.

'What did you do?' queried his fascinated listener.

'Pinned the pesky galoot to the bed with my pickaxe.' The bald statement was uttered as if it was the most natural thing in the world. The Kid shook his head. 'I tell yuh, boy, there was blood everywhere. Janet screamed the place down. I was gonna finish her off in the same way. But somep'n stayed my hand. Then it was too late. The marshal rushed in and arrested me.'

'And so you ended up here,' said Reno.

'I only escaped the gallows because the judge took symapthy on me.' Sagebrush's cratered visage assumed a grim cast. 'Many's the time I've wished he hadn't. This place is no Sunday picnic, as you'll soon discover.'

Reno was given no time to ponder over the old-timer's dismal reflection.

The door crashed open. Three convicts rushed in, grabbed the new inmate and threw him to the floor. He just had time to see Bull Raistrick's leering visage before they set about him with a will. No mercy was shown. And these guys were hardened brawlers. Meaty fists pummelled the victim's body forcing him into a corner.

'What in thunder is this all about?' Reno hollered trying desperately to parry the spate of thudding blows. Blood from numerous cuts flowed down his face which soon resembled a side of raw beef.

'The Ramones were cousins of mine,' snarled the ringleader grimacing. 'This is just a taste of what's comin' your way, mister. So you'd be well advised to watch your back!' Scab Thorndyke stepped back aiming a vicious kick at the victim's exposed kidneys. The brutal assault never connected.

'What's goin' on in here?'

The harsh exclamation came from the Mad Bull, who was standing in the doorway and palming his club with menacing intent. He might have been a brutal sadist, but Raistrick was no fool. A dead man on his hands would lead to awkward questions. 'You skunks are given an hour's recreation after supper, and you go and abuse it. Somebody needs their head crackin'.'

'It were this new jigger, boss,' replied Thorndyke, assuming an air of wronged innocence. 'He stole my snout then attacked me when I protested. The guy's a crazy madman.' The wily convict pulled back in mock fear of his alleged assailant.

'See, boss!' Another of Thorndyke's cronies pointed to a brown wad of tobacco on the floor. 'He tried to push it under the bunk.'

'Yeah!' concurred Thorndyke. 'The sidewinder's a thief as well as a killer.'

An ugly smirk cracked the guard's granite visage. Raistrick was well-satisfied with his little subterfuge. If there was one type of convict that stuck in his craw it was a wanted outlaw figuring he could become a lawman, then reverting back to his old ways when

97

things didn't go according to plan.

Well, Bull Raistrick would make darned sure he got the message loud and clear. This was one skunk whose sentence he would enjoy making pure hell.

'OK, you mealy-mouthed scumbags,' snapped Raistrick, hammering his club on the bars of the cell-door. 'Back to your pits, the lot of yuh. Recreation's cancelled for the rest of the week, thanks to our new guest.'

'And you, Mister high-and-mighty sheriff, can get acquainted with our special penthouse suite. We call it the kennel!'

Raistrick gestured with his cudgel.

'Good luck to you, boy,' was the parting sentiment from Sagebrush, who had maintained a low profile during the bloody altercation. The Kid might have resented the brutal assault on his new cellmate, but there was no way he was about to jeopardize his forth-coming parole board interview.

Reno stumbled outside the cell. A hefty jab from the guard's club sent him spilling towards the outer door. Even following the severe beating, the convict still retained a measure of self-respect. His back stiff-ened. Swinging on his heel, fists clenched, he was all set to deliver a counterblow.

'One more act of defiance from you, pigbrain,' growled the Bull in a flat even tone, his club raised threateningly, 'and I'll have your back opened up on the wheel.' A terse shift of the bullet head was accom-panied by a jerked thrust of the club.

The convict's fiery gaze swung towards the direction

indicated. Reno sucked in a gulp of hot air. The recipient of the grievous attentions of the dreaded appliance was unconscious. He was secured to a wagon wheel, his lacerated back stripped to the bone.

'Figured to answer me back once too often,' commented the pitiless guard with nonchalant disdain. 'That's what happens to critters who fail to show their betters a proper degree of respect. Got the message, lunk head?'

A final heavy push saw Reno disappearing into the shadowy confines of the kennel. The iron door clanged shut over his head.

Through the overhead bars, a twinkling blanket of stars illuminated the night sky. A beautiful tableau to a free man, but to Reno merely a depressing reminder of his brutal incarceration stretching away to the ends of time. Ethereal strips of pale moonlight played across his battered face.

A hiss of indrawn breath came from the far side of the cage.

'Goldarn it, mister! Somebody sure has got it in fer you.'

The remark was wheezed out in a laboured croak. Jackdaw Trent was a thin beanpole who had already been a resident of the Kennel for a week. He had three days still to run.

Reno just lay where he had fallen. He had no strength left to explain. If this was a taster of what was to come, he would rather be dead. His head slumped over a sagging chest. He felt totally bereft of the will to resist any further.

Better just to accept the situation, take his punishment and keep his head down. That was the only way to survive. Otherwise, he was certain that death would be his only visitor. Bull Raistrick was right: buck the system and there was only one winner.

Sleep must have come eventually. But for how long, he had no idea. It was a sharp stab of pure agony that brought the latest incumbent of the kennel stumbling back to full consciousness.

'Aaaaaaagh!' he yelled. His hand reached down to massage what felt like a red-hot needle jabbing into the calf muscle of his left leg. Another searing jolt ripped through his groping hand. 'What in hell's teeth is going on?'

A gleeful bout of chuckling from outside the cage indicated that someone was having fun at his expense.

'Beat the ground with your boots,' urged the other jailbird intently. A note of panic cracked his voice. 'These fellas like to have their bit of fun.'

The laughter from above continued as the two captives swatted and hammered at the scuttling creatures that had invaded their grim quarters. Eventually Bull Raistrick and his buddies got bored and departed to partake of more earthy delights in the fleshpots of Fort Berwick.

It was another fifteen minutes before the last scorpion was blugeoned into submission. Reno breathed deep. His heart was pounding like an overworked steam pump. He looked towards his companion for enlightenment.

'Raistrick does this after he's been at the hard

liquor,' explained Jackdaw Trent. 'Don't worry about being poisoned. These scorpions are harmless but they do pack a nasty wallop.' The skinny convict uttered a maniacal laugh. 'The Mad Bull would soon find himself in here if'n he was to cause the death of a prisoner. Now wouldn't that be a darned shame.'

'So what are you in for?' asked Reno once his heart rate had simmered down to what passed for normal.

'A guard's watch chain had come loose,' explained the cackling thief. 'I just couldn't resist the temptation to relieve him of it. Easy as falling off a log. That's why they call me Jackdaw. Its an illness really. But there ain't no cure. That's why I'm in here and not in hospital.' Reno couldn't help smiling at the convict's devil-may-care attitude. 'Trouble was, the Mad Bull caught me red-handed. So here I am.'

The easy-going manner changed as Jackdaw issued an imperious warning to his fellow incumbent.

'Just make sure you don't challenge the Bull,' he stressed with a wagging finger. 'Otherwise you'll end up kissing the wheel like poor old Sanchez.'

Reno knew that Jackdaw's attitude was all a sham, one man's way of handling the brutal life inside. It could just as easily change to a whining plea once the heat of the day set in. Reno called to mind how the thief had begged for water earlier on. And casually been refused by Raistrick.

The following days passed in a delirious haze of lethargy and heat. Both men could barely summon up the energy to shift their positions. The early pannikin of water soon disappeared, which made the midday ration of bread indigestible until the next delivery at dusk. Kennel sure was an apt name for the cage.

Reno's tongue felt like a lump of hard leather. His throat was raw, any sound little more than a rasping croak. The stamina he possessed was soon eaten away by the body-sapping diet of bread and water. At least no more scorpions appeared. But an even worse play-mate arrived to keep him company on the night following Jackdaw's release.

It was the rattle that alerted the inmate to the fact he was not alone.

A slithering on the earthen floor froze his blood. Then he saw it. The thick swaying body of a full-grown diamondback passed over a beam of moonlight. Reno sat facing the ugly creature, his boots thrust forward to ward off any attack. Twice the rattler made unsuccessful bids to strike at this apparent threat.

Reno knew that it was only a matter of time before the snake got through his meagre defences. His only chance to survive the night was to distract the coiling reptile. Quickly he slipped out of his prison overshirt, and grabbed hold of the heavy steel water holder. Waiting until the snake was coiled into a tight ring with its flat head raised, he threw the garment over the writhing creature.

The snake instantly lunged. But its head was covered by the shirt. With no hesitation, Reno leapt up and hammered the squirming mass, bringing the heavy object down again and again. He only stopped when there was no further movement beneath the overall.

Heart pounding, he gulped air down his dried-up

windpipe. Then he slunk away into the furthest recess of the cage.

There would be no further sleep that night. Although, towards dawn, he must have dropped off.

TEN

BULLDOGGED

'What's been happening in here?'

The gruff demand brought the inmate stumbling out of his brief repose. He pointed to the bloodied rag on the far side of the cage.

'Lift it up!' came the brusque response.

Reno inched over to the tattered remnant and gingerly toed it aside revealing the hideous remains beneath.

'Hey!' called the guard to his colleagues. 'Come take a look at this.' Three guards peered down into the shallow pit.

'Well I never did!' exclaimed Bull Raistrick, casting a cynical gaze at the dead rattlesnake. 'Now I wonder how the devil that critter got hisself locked in there. We gotta be more careful, you guys,' he mockingly chided his fellow custodians. 'Some poor sucker might get bitten. And he wouldn't *fang* us for that now, would he?'

The others howled with laughter at the chief warder's caustic wit.

'You insane bastard!' snarled a wide-eyed Reno Wixx. Realization that Raistrick truly was a deranged butcher who was happy to kill helpless prisoners for his own bestial enjoyment was too much to bear. 'You did this,' he screamed trying to grab the hee-hawing jackass through the cage bars. 'You're nothing but a Mad Bull like everyone says.'

It was a futile gesture. But the insult quickly extinguished the sadistic guard's hilarity. An angry snarl issued from between the yellowed teeth as he smashed his cudgel down on the exposed arm.

'Get this turnip outa there and over to the wheel,' he growled. 'We'll soon see how he likes a taste of the cat ticklin' his back.'

'You sure that's wise, Bull?' cautioned one of the other guards.

'Ugh?' grunted Raistrick. 'You questionin' my orders, Mudlark.'

The other man persisted. 'The governor always wants a report if'n a con is put on the wheel. You know that.'

Raistrick scowled at the guard's hesitancy. 'I can twist that milksop round my little finger.' A feral eye lanced the offending Wilf Mudlark. 'Now get that bastard over there, pronto!'

Mudlark shrugged.

'You're the boss.'

Reno passed out after the tenth stroke. His body was too drained to handle such harsh treatment. It was a blessing in disguise. Raistrick called a halt to the barbarous punishment. Not for the convict's sake. The brutal guard took no pleasure in inflicting pain when the victim was unconscious.

It was evening before Reno finally surfaced.

He was back in the cell block. Sagebrush had bathed his lacerated back and disinfected the wounds with iodine begged from a sympathetic Wilf Mudlark. The guard was no easy touch. He possessed the hard backbone necessary for survival even as a guard in the pen. But even he balked at the savage cruelty displayed by the chief warder.

'Boy, you sure know how to bring the worst out of Bull Raistrick,' remarked the old-timer, dabbing at the tender slash marks.

Reno winced.

Then he remembered. A hard mirthless smile eased aside the bleak aspect.

'At least I didn't give him the satisfaction of crying out,' Reno quipped accepting a thin quirley that his cellmate stuck between the cracked and blistered lips.

It was a week before Convict 1546 was able to resume normal activities. During that time he had been confined to the cell. That was a punishment in itself. So he was more than ready to venture forth into the open air of the main prison courtyard. Reno found himself one of the few spots in the shade.

Atop the far wall, he observed the steady plod of

rifle-bearing sentries. The unrelenting sun beat down on their heads. But at least they could go home at the end of their shift. Unlike this convict who would doubtless resemble old Sagebrush long before he was released.

The bleak notion struck him that escape from this prison was more than likely an impossible dream.

'Got some good news,' offered Sagebrush, sidling up to his cellmate and butting in on his buddy's bleak thoughts.

'Only good news I want is a reprieve,' grumbled Reno, wiping a gritty film of sweat from his face.

The Kid was not affronted by his cellmate's apathetic retort.

'You'll like this,' he insisted. 'Raistrick's been demoted and sent to help supervise the chain gangs.' The old-timer cackled, his bones creaking with merriment. 'Mudlark told me the governor blew his stack. Not about you bein' put on the wheel. Seems he don't cotton to the chief warder bringin' a rattler into his prison. The Mad Bull's nose has been well and truly ringed.' Sagebrush punched the air. 'And he'll be away in the stone quarries for at least a year.'

That development certainly brought the colour back into the morose convict's pallid cheeks.

'Told yuh, didn't I?' hooted Sagebrush jigging about on his stick-thin legs. 'And that ain't all.'

'You mean there's more?' asked the reanimated convalescent with a grin, playing along with the old guy.

'Mudlark's gotten you a job in the kitchens,' gushed

Sagebrush. 'A real cushy number. You sure won't be goin' hungry.' He offered his partner a sly wink. 'And maybe you'll be able to smuggle a few titbits back to your old buddy. For being such a kind-hearted soul an' all.'

Reno's face brightened. This certainly was a change for the better.

Six months passed with little change in the daily routine.

On two more occasions, Scab Thorndyke had attempted to avenge the demise of his outlaw cousins. The first had been broken up by Wilf Mudlark before any serious injury was inflicted on either party. It was the second attempt that resulted in grievous repercussions.

Reno was serving the evening meal when he was grabbed from behind and pinioned by a huge brick wall named Cave Larson. One arm encircled his neck, effectively crushing his windpipe and thus preventing a scream for help. The other jammed the right hand up his back. No matter how much he tried, the man monster had him in a grip of iron.

Cronies of Thorndyke had somehow managed to distract the guards at either end of the refectory. This left the way clear for the prison tyrant to satisfy his unquenched lust for vengeance. The vindictive scheme had been well planned. But he would have to be quick.

Thorndyke leapt over the counter and grabbed a meat cleaver.

'Get his hand down on the chopping block,' ordered the aggressor. A savage grimace clawed the thin lips apart. Two associates grabbed the flexing hand. 'Guys that work in kitchens gotta be mighty careful cutting up chunks of meat or they could easily have an accident.' Thorndyke grinned, moving forward to exact his brutal reprisal.

The cleaver rose.

Bulging eyes followed its trajectory. Reno had a couple of seconds to prevent himself being nicknamed Hooky for evermore. Then he saw it. Just to his left was a large container of bubbling potatoes. His foot immediately shot out, upsetting the balanced pan. In a swirl of hot steam, the boiling water poured out, enveloping the barbaric thug.

Thorndyke was caught completely off guard.

He screamed as the scalding liquid bubbled on his exposed flesh and soaked through the thin clothing. The cleaver fell to the ground. Thorndyke yelped and hollered, jumping about in agony. No less stunned by the sudden change of circumstances were the braggart's sidekicks, who unknowingly released their hold on the intended victim of their skulduggery.

Russ took the opportunity to make himself heard above the clamour.

'Guard! Guard!' he shouted. 'Over here, quick!'

At the same time, he spun round, sinking a bunched fist into the midriff of the gasping Cave Larson. A couple of solid uppercuts to the big man's square jaw followed in rapid succession. No greenhorn at the brawling game, Larson was nonetheless taken by surprise. Another left and a right to the gaping kisser and the Swede went down like a sack of coal.

Seeing their boss no longer in command, the other critters backed off. They were followers, impotent without a leader. Hands were raised in surrender as the guards hurried over. Extreme anger at having been duped ensured that the prisoners received a severe beating as they were herded away.

Reno quickly scooped up the potatoes that were still edible and dropped them back in the pan.

'Next customer, please,' he announced chirpily as though nothing unusual had happened. 'Potatoes are a bit mashed, but beggars can't be choosers. Have your plates ready.'

The other convicts just stared, open-mouthed, agog with amazement. But chow-time in the pen is not to be missed. The line shuffled forward.

In the cell after lockdown, Sagebrush and Reno were lying on their bunks. A friendly moonbeam slanted in through the barred window of the cell. An owl hooting in the distance was answered by its mate. Russ accepted the thin quirley passed down from his partner on the top bunk.

Sagebrush coughed. It was a nervous prelude to the bad tidings he had to impart. Picking his moment, he sucked in a deep breath, then launched forth.

'Heard somep'n on the bush telegraph you need to know,' he said.

There was no answer.

'Bull Raistrick is due back on the block next week.'

He leaned over the side of the bunk, eyeing his partner warily, waiting for the reaction. 'Seems as how he kept his nose clean on the chain gangs, so the governor's let him off the hook.'

Reno aimed a spume of blue smoke at the cracked ceiling.

'And he'll he heaping the blame for all his misfortune on to my shoulders.'

'He'll have to tread carefully,' replied Sagebrush. 'Any more stunts aimed at snuffing out your lights and the governor will hang him out to dry.'

Reno shook his head, unconvinced. 'Time quickly dulls the mind,' he countered with a cynical bite. 'You can bet the governor's forgotten all about me. So long as nobody rocks the boat, he'll turn a blind eye to any underhanded manoeuvres. The Bull could easily arrange a suitable accident.'

'Then we gotta get you out of his way,' pressed the old-timer. A crafty gleam shone in his rheumy eyes as he added, 'And I reckon I know just how we can do it.'

Reno shot him a quizzical frown.

The old guy tapped his nose. 'You leave it to me.' He smirked. The sly wink accompanied a tight grin that revealed teeth yellowed by years of baccy-chewing. 'Got me a few preparations to make afore we get you outa this hellhole.'

ELEVEN

SICKBAY SUBTERFUGE

Grover Sage had been a corpseman during the war. His main task was to retrieve the dead bodies littering the battlefield once the hostilities had moved on. He had also assumed the unlikely role of medical orderly, bandaging wounds and setting broken bones.

When Sage had only three months to serve before his release the governor decided to appoint him prison hospital orderly. It was the nearest that the cons would have to a medic. On previous occasions when serious illnesses had been diagnosed the army doctor from the fort had been summoned. But a guy would have to be on his deathbed before that happened.

The Kid was allowed to sleep over in the sick bay if constant monitoring of a patient was required. A guard looked in every hour to check that everything was all right. There was no chance of the orderly assisting an escape as the inmate was always chained to the bed overnight.

But the old reprobate had surreptitiously lifted the key during the early hours when the guard was asleep. After making a mould of the key in a bar of soap he had arranged for Jackdaw Trent to have a spare made in the prison workshop.

Early the next morning, Sagebrush hammered on the door of his cell.

'Guard! Guard!' he yelled, the hoarse clamour laden with panic. 'Open up quick!'

'What in hell's name you makin' all that racket for, Sagebrush?' snapped a testy custodian. 'Stow yer gaff else I'll have you in the kennel.'

'It's my buddy here,' replied the concerned prisoner.

'What about him?'

'He's got. . . .'

'Well, y'ol' windbag, out with it. What's he got?' came back the impatient rejoinder.

Sagebrush paused, deliberately building the tension.

'*Cholera*!' he hissed.

That single word had the impact of a punch in the guts. It was what every governor dreaded. The deadly disease could spread like wildfire in the close confines of a prison.

The guard flung open the door standing back, his rifle at the ready.

'H-how d'yuh know it's cholera?' he burbled, mouth

hanging open.

'I'm the hospital orderly, ain't I?' snapped the convict. 'I knows cholera when I sees it. We gotta him into quarantine, *rapido*.'

The guard hesitated. This dire occurrence outside his experience. What should he do?

Sagebrush pressed home the imperative message

'Yuh don't want to be responsible for the spread a killer like this, do yuh, boss?' he urged. 'Isolation the only way to stop it spreading. Then you'd be hero. The guy who saved the Dakota pen.'

'What's goin' on out there?' hollered a muted vo from the next cell.

'Cut yer howlin'!' rasped the guard, hammering the door with the butt end of his rifle. 'Ain't concern of your'n.'

The interruption was enough to jerk him i action.

'All right. Get him over to the sick bay. Sooner turkey is locked up in solitary the better.'

The guard was sweating as Sagebrush manhandl the sick convict out of the cell. Reno groaned alor eager to play his part to the full. He stretched ou hand to the hovering custodian who fearfully shra away to avoid any contact with the virulent disease.

Bad news always travels fast. Even before the mid bell for chow, cholera was on everyone's lips. Only Sagebrush Kid was allowed access to the infect convict. He smiled to himself. It was just as h planned.

The isolation room was located on the outside v

of the prison. The windows were barred but that was no hindrance. Somehow, Jackdaw Trent had managed to acquire a hacksaw. Sagebrush never questioned his buddy's methods. He was a scrounger *par excellence.* And that was all that mattered.

After the hospital guard had departed, the crafty con set about cutting through the bars. It was tough work. Reno spelled him every half-hour. After removing sheets from two of the remaining beds, he tied them together ready for the escape that night. Four sheets were required to provide a sufficient length to reach the ground two floors below. Then he hid the improvised rope under one of the beds.

Little was said. Each prayed that the moon would see fit to remain hidden under a thick blanket that night.

Both men knew what needed to be done. They were constantly on the alert for the guard's return each hour. Luckily, he never entered the room. Fear of the contagion was a powerful deterrent. This was what Sagebrush had counted on. It left him free to make preparations for Reno's clandestine departure without fear of discovery.

Afternoon slowly passed into evening. Tensions mounted in the sick bay as the moment of truth drew near. As darkness enfolded the prison, the guard ordered Sagebrush to secure the patient to the bed. The orderly then retired to his own temporary quarters.

Once the guard had left, he crept back into the sick bay and freed his partner.

Reno quickly cut through the last sliver of metal holding the bars in place. Then he retrieved the sheet rope and fed it out of the window, down the outside wall, tying off the upper end to the remaining window bar. The final act was to lay the bolster in the bed to give the illusion of a sleeping body when the guard made his hourly check.

'This is it, boy,' whispered Sagebrush. His voice fizzled with the strain. 'You ready?'

Reno nodded. No sense jawing too much. They both knew that sound carried further at night.

Their eyes met. The warm glow of comradeship and trust rippled through the tense atmosphere as Reno gripped the older-timer's bony shoulder.

'You sure you don't wanna come with me?' he asked for the umpteenth time.

'As I told yuh before,' sighed his partner. ''I'm due outa here in a couple of months.'

'But you could be blamed for this caper,' stressed Reno firmly.

'There ain't no proof that I had anything to do with it,' Sagebrush insisted. 'I'll just say you planned the whole thing on your ownsome. I was as surprised at the escape as everyone else.' Then he pushed the younger man towards the window. 'Now get goin',' he urged. 'You've got six hours before I make the discovery that you've flown the nest.'

They clasped hands.

Then Reno was shimmying down the knotted-sheet rope. He gave thanks to a higher authority that it was indeed a dark night. The chirruping of crickets in a nearby stand of cottonwoods was the only sound to disturb the oppressive silence.

But the hand of a scheming devil was about to enter the fray.

Unknown to either of the conspirators, Bull Raistrick had arrived back at the prison early. On hearing of the outbreak of cholera and the identity of the supposed carrier, his cynical nature immediately sensed a deception was afoot. Without any vacillation, he hustled over to the sickbay.

Peering through the spyhole in the door, he perceived the supposed patient asleep in bed. All seemed in order. Now was his chance to finish this conniving skunk once and for all. A pillow over the face and nobody would suspect a thing. Blackfoot Reno had died in his sleep.

Gingerly he unlocked the door and crept over to the bed. A puzzled frown furrowed his heavy brow. Something wasn't right here. The shape of the body was too straight. Suspecting foul play, he whipped back the covering blanket and gasped aloud.

The bed was empty.

Where had the bastard gone? Then he saw the missing bars carelessly stuck into place with soap and a sheet tied to the end one. Poking his head through the window, he saw Reno halfway down the wall.

A low growl emerged from his taut jaw. Raistrick palmed his revolver and thumbed back the hammer to full cock. Sharp clicks ripped through the stifling air, alerting the fugitive. Reno automatically looked up.

The Mad Bull's leering visage stared down at him.

'Now I can kill you legally,' he chortled, leaning ⊂
of the window. 'Blackfoot Reno – shot while trying
escape.'

The runaway stared death in the face as the guar⟨
finger tightened on the trigger. But no shots rang o⟨
A stifled croak emerged from the guard's open mou
as his body disappeared from view.

A few minutes later it was replaced by that of t⟨
Sagebrush Kid.

'Reckon I'd better join you after all, Reno,'
mumbled, climbing out and scuttling crablike do⟨
the rope.

Reno chafed at the bottom until his partner arriv⟨

'What happened up there?' he muttered.

The old-timer shook his head as he bent low a⟨
hurried over to the cover afforded by the nearby c
tonwoods.

Breath held in check, they both listened intently

Silence still enfolded the night.

'Raistrick must have came back early,' the old g
gasped out in answer to his sidekick's questioni⟨
regard, 'and suspected somep'n was up. He did⟨
spot me over in the corner of the room.' The old g
gulped hard, the ancient ticker beating a rapid tatt⟨
on his ribcage. His head fell forward as the full imp⟨
of his recent actions rumbled to the fore.

'Easy there, old-timer,' soothed Reno.

'Had to skewer him else he'd have gunned y⟨
down in cold blood,' Sagebrush averred.

'Is he dead?'

'As a boot hill fandango,' came back the qui⟨

118

retort. 'Didn't have any choice in the matter when I saw him leering down at yuh from that window. At least the pesky critter won't be troublin' any other poor cons in this world.' The Kid raised his head and fastened a troubled look on his partner. 'Seems like we're stuck with each other for a spell longer.' A rueful smile broke across the grizzled countenance. 'Don't mind, do yuh, boy'?'

'Glad to have you along, Kid,' replied Reno, returning the smile. 'Now I suggest we get out of this place while we got the chance.'

'You'd better take charge of this,' said Sagebrush, handing a shiny Colt Peacemaker to his buddy. 'Figured that Raistrick won't be needin' it again. And a hogleg might come in handy.'

'You ain't just a perty face, are you, mister?' There was a hint of respect in the remark. The old guy had done well. It was just bad luck that Bull Raistrick had shown up when he did.

One behind the other they headed down an easy grade towards the distant outline of dwarf willows lining the banks of the Missouri. At that point the river was over a half-mile wide and flowing at a fast lick. Reno shook his head. It was impossible to cross. And from what he recalled of the gruelling trek east from Del Norte, the only feasible crossing point was at Fort Pierre.

And that was three days' ride to the north. But they were on foot, so it was out of the question anyway. The Pierre ferry would be the first place to which the pursuers would head. Their only chance was to head south in the opposite direction and hope to find a suitable crossing when dawn broke.

Scrabbling along the wooded banks of the mighty Missouri in the dark was tough going, especially for old Sagebrush. It soon became apparent that they would have to rest up. Sheer exhaustion following the traumatic experiences of the last few hours caused both of them to fall instantly into a deep sleep.

The sun was already well above the eastern horizon when Reno opened his eyes. But something else had woken him. For some moments his brain was too sluggish to take in his surroundings. Rubbing the grit from his eyes, he sat up.

Then he heard it.

The baying of hounds.

And they were not far back down the river. Raistrick's body must have been discovered. The pursuit of the fugitives was in full swing. With one of their own knifed to death in the furtherance of an escape, nothing would satisfy the authorities until the perpetrators were apprehended and subjected to the full rigor of the law. And that would mean a certain necktie party for them both.

'Wake up, old-timer,' urged Reno shaking his buddy awake. 'We need to get going. Hear that?' he cocked an ear to the steadily increasing tumult. 'They've gotten the dogs on our tail.'

The two men struggled onward. But after a half-hour it became readily apparent that the dogs and their handlers were getting closer.

Sagebrush stopped. His ageing lungs felt ready to burst. Wheezing like a broken concertina, he slumped to the ground.

'I . . . can't . . . go on any more,' he panted. 'Leave me . . . here with the gun. I'll hold 'em off while you get a head start.'

'There's no way that I'm leaving you.' Reno was adamant. There was a steadfast persistence in his grainy look. 'We're partners who stick together. I can always carry you on my back.'

The old man gripped Reno's shirt. Gathering himself, he aimed a withering glare at his young buddy.

'Listen up, mister,' he growled. 'Stay here and we're both crowbait. There's six bullets in that pistol. Enough for me to stall 'em and let you give them turkeys the slip.' His determined gaze showed no fear or regret. 'I'm an old jasper who ain't never amounted to much. You've got your whole life ahead of yuh. How else are yuh gonna pay back that doubled-crossin' skunk?'

Sagebrush fell back, his breathing laboured. Reno could see that he was well and truely whacked. And that what he said made sense.

'This is my last opportunity to do some good,' urged the stricken convict. 'One final chance to help a buddy out.' A pleading look softened the hard exterior of the old man's wizened face. 'You wouldn't deny me that now, would yuh, Reno?'

The yapping grew louder. Reno could even make

out the holler of raised voices. They were no more than a half-hour behind.

He held out his hand. Sagebrush gripped it tightly. A smile cracked the heavily lined contours.

'Now git goin'.' he ordered. 'And good luck.'

Reno handed over the pistol.

'You make every shot count,' he stressed, a single teardrop etching a path down his tanned face.

The old man waved him away. Fifty yards along the uneven bank, the fugitive paused, turning to survey his backtrail. Old Sagebrush was settling himself behind a log in readiness for his final battle. A lump formed in Reno's throat, knowing that his buddy was about to make the ultimate sacrifice. He made himself a promise that it would not be in vain. A vow that entailed his accomplishing a clean getaway.

Tense and alert, Reno listened intently as he continued along the riverbank. Fearful tension racked his brain. Another half-hour passed before the first shots broke the spell. Desultory at first, all too soon the crash of gunfire told its own story. But with only six bullets, Sagebrush could not hold out for long.

Blood-curdling growls from the attacking hounds brought a flood of tears to the distraught man. He slumped to his knees, head in hands. The bent form presented the very picture of dejection.

But only for a moment.

This ain't no way to behave, he told himself, shaking the melancholic grip from stiffened limbs. The old guy gave his life for you to escape. Least you can do is make that loss worth while. A fresh surge of determination coursed through the runaway's body. He carried on, keeping a close eye on the river and praying for a suitable crossing point.

TWELVE

UNEXPECTED ENCOUNTER

The relentless pace continued throughout the morning. The barking hounds were now barely audible. A bleak smile of satisfaction split Reno's grim countenance. But they would not give up, doggedly following the scent until they ran him to ground.

He sat down, resting his weary frame against a tree trunk. The desire for sleep was overwhelming. His eyelids drooped.

Then a low rustling sound assailed his ears. An alien noise that could only be man-made. Surely the pursuing gang had not caught up this soon? Quickly Reno scrambled behind some nearby rocks, and waited, his body wound tighter than a watch spring. Within a minute a shadow crossed the trail. He let it pass before leaping out.

The pair went down hard. With surprise on his side, Reno managed to get atop the other. His left hand clamped across the guy's throat, the right drew back to deliver a heavy blow to the lantern jaw.

'Hold on, mister!' The alarmed exclamation stayed his hand momentarily. 'I ain't part of that darned posse. See here,' he pressed on, urgently jabbing his free hand at his striped overshirt. 'We're both escaped cons.'

Reno loosened his grip, although he still remained keenly alert, just in case this was a trick.

'So where did you spring from?' enquired Reno, not deigning to conceal his suspicions regarding this guy's sudden appearance. 'A mite strange if'n you ask me.'

'I escaped from the chain gang three days ago after trying to slug Bull Raistrick,' said the new arrival. Reno gave a sigh of understanding. 'The louse promised to open my back on the wheel.' A plain shiver of terror rippled through the guy's taut frame at the recollection. 'Some of the others staged a fight to draw the attention of the guards. Then I hid in a ditch until nightfall. Thought I'd gotten clean away. I heard them dogs this morning and figured they was on my tail. I never cottoned that some other con would have done a runner at the same time.'

'Me and my buddy escaped from the pen last night,' replied Reno with grudging acceptance of the guy's explanation.

The other man gave him a puzzled look.

'Where's your partner, then?'

'You heard that gunfire back aways?' The guy nodded. 'Well, that was old Sagebrush giving me the chance to make a clean break. He killed Raistrick during the breakout and commandeered his pistol.' He went on to explain the circumstances of his own escape.

A ponderous silence followed.

'I promised Sagebrush that I wouldn't let them take me alive,' added Reno sombrely.

'Then what we waitin' fer,' spurred the other. 'That is if'n you don't mind company.' The ex-chainy eyed Reno expectantly.

'Sure thing, mister,' said Reno. 'Be glad of it. The name's Blackfoot Reno.'

'I'm Arby Duggan,' he responded holding out a hand. 'One time bank-robber and hold-up man.' He smiled. 'It all went wrong when I tried to go solo and hold up a stage on the Deadwood trail outside Rapid City. Too many darned eyes needed fer that caper.'

Reno was about to grasp the preferred appendage when his eyes gaped wide, fastening on to a tattoo revealed on Duggan's exposed forearm. He had seen that picture before somewhere. And the name – Arby Duggan – seemed vaguely familiar.

Then it struck him like a thump in the back from an angry longhorn.

The guy's mugshot was pinned up on the studio wall. It was the last picture he had processed before his arrest. The image now came back to him clear as the moonlit sky.

It was the same man. The same lean weasel-like

face. But most distinctive of all was the pattern of a tat-
tooed anchor and chain on his forearm.

'Seems like we've met before, Arby,' murmured
Reno, while subjecting the grinning outlaw to a keen
scrutiny.

The little guy raised a quizzical eyebrow.

'Remember Del Norte and that failed bank job?'

Now it was Duggan's turn to gaze open-mouthed.

A wavering finger pointed. 'You're that jigger that
gunned down my pards and had me locked up,' he
said, not quite knowing how to react to this mind-
numbing declaration. 'I recall you went under the
handle of Russ Wikeley then. So how come—?'

'It's a long story,' interjected Reno, standing up.
'I'll fill you in once we're in the clear. First thing is to
find some place to cross the river. That's the only way
we're gonna shake off them damn hounds.'

Duggan voiced no objection, and they set off. Once
again Reno was partnered by an outlaw. Would this
one prove as resourceful as old Sagebrush?

Only time would tell.

An hour passed. The increasing clamour to their
rear was alarming. Fatigue, compounded by weeks on
a squalid diet was measurably slowing the pace of the
two fugitives. Cast afoot, they stood little chance of
outwitting men on horseback with dogs. Capture was
inevitable unless they found a way across the river.

As they rounded a bend Reno spotted a pair of
hunters up ahead. They were crouched over the
river's edge, clutching hold of fishing poles. And close
by was a canoe. The runaways ducked out of sight.

Here was their chance. These guys would have every-thing they needed: clothes, guns and, most important, a means of reaching the far side of the Missouri and freedom.

Exercising due care to avoid alerting the two hunters, Reno led the way forward. The hunters were concentrating on their fishing lines, hunkered down at the water's edge. More significant, they were facing away from the approaching bushwhackers. Luckily, their gear was higher up the riverbank. Reno quickly commandeered their guns.

The first the two unsuspecting fishermen knew of their not being alone was a pistol jammed into each of their necks.

'Just take it nice and easy, fellas,' hissed Reno, 'and you won't get hurt. All we want is your goods and a quick paddle to the other side of the river.'

The hunters were stunned into silence on realizing they had been suckered by two escaped convicts. Dropping the fishing poles, their arms reached high.

It was the older of the hunters who recovered first.

'You guys escaped from the pen?' he asked, unfazed by the sudden change in circumstances. The striped jerseys were an obvious giveaway.

'Hurry it up, you critters,' Arby snapped, ignoring the question as he jabbed the gun forward with threat-ening menace. 'Off with them duds. We ain't got time for no palaver.' The ululating racket from the approaching posse was growing in volume.

'Don't worry none, boys,' announced one hunter chirpily. 'Me and Red here won't cause you no bother.' The ginger mophead bobbed in agreement. 'We've crossed swords with the law many a time. I'd be obliged though if'n you'd leave the fish we caught. Some mighty fine trout in that there net.'

Within five minutes the two hunters had been tethered by their own fishing lines and the fugitives were pushing off from the riverbank. Oars dug deep into the swirling torrent as they paddled out into midstream. It was no easy matter to reach the far bank without being swept downstream. Fortunately, at this point the turbulent flow had lessened to such a degree that they only lost fifty yards.

Upon landing, they hid the canoe in the reeds and pushed inland. Still on foot, it was imperative that they acquired some mounts to ensure a clean getaway. The shadows lengthened into dusk without their encountering another human soul. An old cabin, long since abandoned to the elements, offered shelter for the night.

Over a welcome supper of bacon and beans washed down by a gallon of steaming Arbuckles, Reno outlined his sorry tale. A half-bottle of rotgut whiskey helped loosen his new partner's tongue as to his own adventures following the first jailbreak from Del Norte. The flickering embers of the dying fire danced a merry gig as Duggan concluded his story.

'Might have figured it was that louse Stoner that stitched you up,' sighed the outlaw, puffing on a black cheroot. 'Only when I threatened to disclose his scheme to rob the bank did he agree to help me escape. And even then he refused to give me a grubstake. Seems like you and me both got a grudge agin that critter.'

Reno stiffened on learning the grim truth about the Del Norte bank job. Although he'd suspected that Jim Stoner had had a hand in it, there was no proof. Now he had a witness. Then his eyes clouded over. Why should this guy agree to give evidence against his old boss, knowing that he himself was implicated and likely to serve time for it?

But if Duggan backed his play to expose the crafty rat, that would go in his favour. And with Russell Wikeley installed as the legitimate law-enforcement officer, any past offences could surely be pardoned on his recommendation.

He put the proposition to Duggan.

'It would mean you going back to Del Norte with me and laying yourself open to arrest,' Reno submitted hesitantly. 'There's no guarantee that we can force Stoner's hand and expose him for the felonious double-dealer that he is.' Reno sucked air through clenched teeth. 'And he'll have Newcombe installed as sheriff by now. So it's gonna be a tough job to oust him.'

Reno fastened a candid yet sanguine eye on the outlaw. 'If'n we succeed, I will make it my business to get you set up with a fresh start.'

He paused to give the other man chance to digest the import of his offer. Duggan had been all ears. There was nothing he wanted more than to erase his owlhoot ways. This was his chance to do just that.

'You got yourself a deal,' he said. 'So what do I call

you? Is it Blackfoot Reno or Russ Wikeley?'

The photographer smiled. He gazed into the glimmering tongue of flame before replying.

'Reno Wixx is dead. Russ Wikeley has been given a new lease of life.'

As dawn broke the two escapees pushed on. Following the direction of the sun, they headed west. Broken landscape surrendered to rolling grassland which offered little in the way of concealment. But at least they would be given advance warning of any approaching posse.

However, it soon became apparent that without horses they were unlikely to get far. And food was running low. The hunters had only carried enough for a few days. Russ managed to shoot a couple of rabbits to augment their meagre rations. But after three days, they were down to their last meal. If something didn't turn up soon, they were done for.

Then, out of the blue rode a man straddling a large bay mare. He was herding a group of mustangs some half-mile distant, parallel to the direction of the fugitives. And he was moving at a fair canter. Another few minutes and the small party would have disappeared.

An immediate decision whether to attract his attention was needed. The guy could prove friendly and accommodating, or otherwise. Should they take the chance? Russ arrowed his partner with a quizzical look. Duggan responded with a curt nod. So Russ removed the old Navy Colt from his waist band and blasted the two remaining shots into the air.

The sharp cracks echoed across the waving sea
green.

The rider hauled rein. Quickly he slid from t
saddle, removed a Winchester carbine from its bc
and dropped to one knee. On the wide open plains
the frontier a man shot first and asked questions lat
It was a matter of survival.

To indicate their peaceful intent, Russ waved
grubby white cloth in the air. Both men stood, han
raised. Was this the end of the line? Keeping the ri
cocked and ready, the wrangler mounted up a
approached with due caution. His eyes never left t
two travellers.

'You fellas lost?' he enquired charily.

'We were robbed by a couple of escaped convi
down on the Missouri,' Russ improvised, exuding
confidence that was pure illusion. 'They took all o
goods and left us afoot.'

'You're a lifesaver, mister,' interposed Dugga
latching on to his partner's fanciful story. 'We ran c
of food yesterday.'

The wrangler was a grizzled old guy with a head
iron grey hair that stuck out from beneath a wic
brimmed plainsman hat. Although on the wrong si
of fifty, he carried himself with solid assurance.

'The name's Cal Mason,' he said, appearing
accept the story at face value. 'I run the Leaning
horse ranch in the next valley. We supply mustangs
the army at Fort Beswick.'

'We'd be obliged for some grub and a couple
them mounts if'n you've a mind,' suggested Ru

imbuing the request with a placatory tone. 'Me and my buddy here will be more'n willing to work for them.'

Mason surveyed the pair of disreputable travellers with a jaundiced gaze from beneath heavily beetled eyebrows. He considered himself to be a firm judge of character. That sixth sense had always served him well in the past. And these guys sounded genuine.

'OK,' he said eventually. 'You got yourself a deal. Work off the debt and we'll call it quits.'

'Much obliged, Mr Mason,' replied Russ breezily. 'You won't regret it.'

THIRTEEN

EQUINE INTERLUDE

The log cabin and outbuildings that comprised the Leaning M were sited on a raised terrace of the White River, a tributary of the mighty Missouri. Two weeks into their stint of work, Russ was enjoying every minute of the hard physical labour. At first it had been tough going after the brutal and debilitating regime of the penitentiary. But experience of handling wild broncs stood him in good stead. And he relished the challenge of man against beast. It was dangerous but rewarding work.

Most interesting of all, however, was the presence of Cal Mason's daughter. Laura was a shy retiring girl. Pretty as a picture with long auburn tresses that she pinned up into a swishing ponytail, the young girl had barely spoken a word to the newcomers. She served

134

their meals, and undertook the basic domestic chores with an easy grace.

On more than one occasion Russ had caught the girl eyeing him up, discreetly but with a stirring in her breast she found difficult to comprehend. The emotion was both exciting and frightening. A wide smile from the handsome new bronc-buster was met with blushing cheeks and a flustered attempt to ignore the welcome attention.

For Laura was courting a labourer off the neighbouring dirt farm.

Not the brightest button in the box, Rubin Tubbs nonetheless had quickly cottoned to the fact that his sweetheart was casting her net elsewhere. And he was none too pleased. Things came to a head one Saturday afternoon.

Tubbs had come over to visit Laura and caught her mooning over the new wrangler who was showing off his horse-riding skills to the appreciative audience. The farmhand scowled. He had to do something or the lovely Laura would be lost for ever.

After Russ had finished his demonstration and taken the feisty quarter horse for a rub down, Rubin tackled the girl over her infatuation.

'Ain't no business of your'n who I favour,' snapped the girl, swishing her hair and prancing off like a young colt. 'You got no hold over me.'

'We're gonna be married, ain't we?' whined the blustering youth.

'That's for me to decide.' Laura threw Tubbs a disdainful look that struck the suitor right between the eyes. 'And I don't figure you're the right one for me.'

Tubbs uttered a wolfish growl. His hand shot out and roughly grabbed a hold of the girl, tearing her dress.

'It's that darned bronco-buster, ain't it?' he hollered, roughly shaking her. 'You've gone and cast yer cap at him.'

'Take your dirty hands off me, Rubin Tubbs, and leave me be,' Laura cried out. She was frightened. This was a new side to the farm boy that she had not previously encountered.

Russ had heard the commotion. He appeared just in time to prevent the bully from slapping the girl. A quick left and a right to the kid's jaw sent him sprawling on the ground.

'You heard the lady, mister,' Russ snarled. 'She don't want you here. So I suggest you leave now.'

Tubbs scrambled away from the looming attacker. Rubbing a trace of blood from his mouth he snarled, 'I'm goin' but you ain't heard the last of this. Neither of yuh!'

That was the start of a relationship that blossomed over the next two weeks. Cal Mason was not unaware of the attentions his daughter was receiving from the young wrangler. Nor was he averse to the liaison.

But Rubin Tubbs was not a man to be thwarted. Thoughts of retaliation festered in his soul. It came when he saw a Wanted poster pinned up outside the marshal's office in the nearby town of Bell Forge.

Two men had escaped from the penitentiary and were still on the loose. Most important for Rubin was the reward on offer. With 500 dollars, he could put down a deposit on a spread of his own. Then Laura would surely come a-running.

The Masons, together with their new wrangler and his partner, were at breakfast the following morning when there was a firm knock on the door. It startled those at the table, none of whom had heard the approach of any visitors.

Laura got up to answer the door.

Marshal Butch Daggart stepped inside and removed his hat. He was accompanied by a deputy. Each man carried a rifle, their other hands poised above holstered revolvers.

'This a social call, Marshal?' asked Cal Mason, chewing on a corndog.

'Afraid not,' muttered Daggart, fastening a suspicious eye on to the two seated ranch hands. 'It's been reported that two escaped convicts are hiding out on this ranch.' Deadpan faces, unmoving and set firm, stared back at the hovering lawman. Neither gave any hint that their nerves were strung tight as drawn bow strings.

The deputy casually sidled to the rear of where Duggan was seated.

'Any descriptions of these dudes?' Mason responded easily.

'One is reckoned to be a rangy clean-shaven jasper who has teamed up with an old wizened fella.' Russ swallowed hard at this revelation, briefly catching his partner's eye. 'Both are desperate killers. Anybody who comes across them is advised to be very careful.'

The lawman paused. 'You ain't come across these jaspers, have yuh, Cal?'

'I sure have,' averred the rancher with blunt emphasis.

Russ's hand dropped below the table, gripping a sheathed Bowie knife. His other fingered the course stubble hiding his features. If necessary he was pre-pared to fight his way out of this predicament. Although such action would be a last resort. No way did he want to place his benefactors in any danger.

'The fellas you mention came through here two weeks back,' continued Mason. 'A young guy and a grey-bearded jigger that looked older than Methuselah. I gave 'em some food and they left. Only later did I find they'd gone and stolen my two best mustangs.' He sighed shaking his head. 'Can't trust nobody these days.'

Relaxation of the tense atmosphere was palpable.

'In that case I'll let you good folks finish your meal,' concluded the lawman.

'Hope you catch them no-accounts, Marshal,' called Mason as the two lawmen departed.

Russ looked at his partner.

'Much obliged for that, Cal,' murmured a some-what chastened Russ Wikeley. 'Seems like we owe you an explanation.'

'I'm all ears, boys,' replied the rancher. His expres-sion was stony. 'And it better be good.'

Laura was likewise eager to hear whether her decla-ration of love for the young man had been misplaced.

An hour later, following a detailed outline of the

entire saga, a broad smile broke across the rancher's crusty visage. He held out a gnarled paw.

'I believe you boys,' he said. 'But my advice is to quit this territory pronto. It's clear to me that Rubin Tubbs is the one that betrayed you. And he ain't gonna be well pleased when he learns that you're still here, and courting his gal.

'You've earned your keep and more during the last month,' continued the rancher. 'Laura will prepare you some vittles, and you can take your pick of the mounts.' Then he reached into a pocket. 'And here's some wages. It ain't much.'

'That's mighty generous of you, Cal,' answered Russ. 'We really appreciate what you've done for us.'

'Just make darned sure you clear your name over in Del Norte.'

A half-hour later, the mounts were ready, the saddle-bags packed with two weeks' supplies. Enough to get them back to Del Norte.

'Time we was gettin' on the trail,' called Arby to his partner.

Russ was dragging his feet. The last thing he wanted was to leave Laura. But there was no other option. Retribution and a final account beckoned.

'Once this business with Diamond Jim Stoner is finished, I'll be back,' he promised, kissing her on the lips. Laura responded with a passionate ardour she had never experienced before. She wanted it to go on for ever. At last they parted. 'Then I'll make this union legal. What do you say to becoming the wife of a bronc-rider?'

139

She hugged him close. 'Just get back here in one piece, y'hear?'

The two partners had ridden over a mile before Russ felt able to swing round in the saddle and cast a watery eye to his rear.

Laura was still there. She had not moved. Then her arm lifted. He could almost hear the whispered sentiment, 'Until we meet again.'

FOURTEEN

TAKING STOCK

Heading steadily westward, the intrepid pair followed the left bank of the White River until its rapidly diminishing flow eventually faded out in the barren wilderness known as the Badlands. The sudden change from flat grassland to sterile mountain remnants was eye-popping. Old riverbeds that looked as if they had been scored by the claws of some giant leviathan ensured that travel across this wasteland was fraught with danger.

A more inhospitable landscape was difficult to imagine. Mesquite, thorn and cholla cactus predominated. The dusty white of heavily alkaline crusts soaked up any moisture, so that surface water was a distinct rarity.

The only way to handle this brutal terrain was with speed and skill.

After five days of tortuous meanderings amidst the

141

harsh landscape, the sight of pine woods heralding the start of the Black Hills was like striking gold. As they entered the valley of Blacktail Gulch, rain clouds gathered. A steady downpour soon hammered on yellow slickers as the two partners pressed onward towards their goal.

Russ drew his mount to a halt at the edge of Del Norte. His brooding eyes scanned the burgeoning township. Much had changed during his enforced absence. Tents had given way to more permanent structures. New houses occupied the lower slopes of the valley. He idly surmised which one Jim Stoner had commissioned. No doubt the most lavish.

Nudging their horses forward at a steady walk, the two riders were glad of the thick mantle of cloud swathing the valley sides. Tendrils of white mist drifted down from the heights above. Most folks were indoors. Russ tugged down the brim of his sodden hat, concealing his face. Not that anybody would recognize this mean-eyed drifter now. Gone was the easy-going photographer who always had a winning smile. The jasper now occupying his body suggested an infinitely more ruthless persona.

An angry snarl ground in his throat like broken glass as he surveyed his old photographic premises. The Magic Eye Picture Studio was no more. It had been replaced by a garish music-hall theatre. Large posters advertised the latest acts imported from Denver and beyond.

The current artist treading the boards was a certain *Miss Flossy Perkins – exotic dancer accompanied by her slip-*

pery assistant, Peter the Python. Exotic indeed mused Arby Duggan, licking his lips. After being in the can for a spell, the outlaw was eager to view the coming entertainment.

'All in good time, Arby,' cautioned Russ reading his partner's lurid thoughts. 'First we have to make sure that Stoner and his crew get the message that they're finished in Del Norte.'

During their protracted journey from the Leaning M ranch, the pair had discussed how they were going to stymie Stoner's ambitions and clear Russ's name. A tentative plan had been thrashed out.

'First off though,' suggested Russ, 'I reckon we've earned ourselves a couple of beers.'

'Now you're talking, boss.' His partner grinned as they pointed their mounts to the nearest hitching post.

'But not that one.' Russ jabbed a gloved hand towards the Panhandle. 'Stoner and his minions hang out there.'

Having tied up, they pushed through the doors of the Blue Pearl. It was quiet inside. The bartender was idly polishing glasses. Only one man was at the bar. Hunched over a glass of whiskey, Russ immediately recognized his old friend Dewlap Jenson.

'You get the drinks,' Russ whispered to his partner, 'and bring them over to that booth yonder. Then invite the guy at the bar to join us.'

Arby gave him a slanted look, then shrugged before sashaying over to the bar.

When Jenson arrived Russ was staggered at his old

buddy's dishevelled appearance. Whisps of thin g
hair hung down across a face ravaged by hard liqu
He was thin as a rake, the gaunt face drawn and blo
less. The newspaperman tried not to show his disr
as his old buddy greeted him. But Jenson was
fooled. He knew the score. At that moment, howe
his concern was for Russ Wikeley.

'Don't let any of Stoner's crew recognize you,'
urged peering around to ensure that nobody
paying them unwanted attention. 'That guy has
town sewn up tighter than a dancer's girdle. I gu
you must have some kind of plan now that you
back?'

'You still running the *Tribune*?' asked Russ ho
fully, avoiding a reply to Jenson's question.

Jenson shook his head. 'Stoner threatened to b
me out if'n I didn't sell up. It was a miserly offer.
I didn't have much choice once you got sent dov
Then he perked up some. 'Still got one of my pres
though.'

'That's what I was hoping,' said Russ. 'You wan
get your self-respect back I assume?'

'Darned tootin' I do,' replied Jenson throu
gritted teeth. A fresh gleam of anticipation for a 1
beginning was resurrected in his bony features.

'Then this is what I want you to do.'

An hour later, Jenson stood up to leave. He push
aside the bottle of hooch that Russ offered.

'I'm off the hard stuff until this business is c
cluded,' he asserted with a firm conviction. The g
pallor had disappeared. A fresh resolve showed in

upright bearing. 'One way or another.' The buoyant mood darkened for a moment. 'Sorry to have to tell you this, Russ,' Dewlap apologized, his rheumy eyes narrowing, 'but Eleanor teamed up with Stoner soon after you'd been sent down. She couldn't even wait for the dust to settle.'

Russ's response was an shrug. 'Always figured she was one to follow the main chance.'

Mid-afternoon found a weak sun nudging aside the thick belt of cloud. Steam rose from the waterlogged street as Arby Duggan sauntered casually down towards the sheriff's office. The name on the new sign read *Charles T Newcombe – Sheriff of Del Norte and the Upper Deadwood.*

Ensuring that he was unobserved, Duggan knocked on the heavy oak door.

A grunted reply followed which he assumed was a summons to enter. The lawman was slumped in a chair, his booted legs resting on the scarred desk top. In his hand was a half-empty whiskey bottle. He was clearly the worse for wear, and it was not even three o'clock.

Newcombe did not recognize the visitor. Duggan had grown a thick moustache and his long curly black hair concealed much of his face.

The sheriff shot the newcomer a suspicious glower.

'What d'yuh want?' he slurred, taking another swig from the bottle. 'Make it double quick cos I'm a busy man.'

'I can see that, Sheriff,' sneered Duggan. 'So I won't

beat about the bush. Got some news concerning a wanted man that will net us both a hefty reward if'n you've a mind.'

Mention of a bounty perked up the bleary-eyed tin star.

'You got some information then you're duty bound to spill it,' ordered Newcombe, struggling to his feet. He set his hat straight and hitched up his gunbelt, trying unsuccessfully to assume the guise of a tough lawman.

Duggan kept a straight face.

'I know where you can find the wanted outlaw called Blackfoot Reno,' declared the outlaw. 'If'n you recall, he's the varmint who was sentenced to twenty years for murder and robbery. But he escaped from the pen and is heading this way for revenge against those who framed him.'

Newcombe might have been somewhat the worse for drink, but he was no fool. 'How come you know so much, mister?' he said accusingly. 'Could be you're in cahoots with this critter.'

Duggan scoffed at the suggestion.

'It's my business to know such things,' he emphasized brusquely. He threw down the old faded dodger. 'Get my drift?'

'A bounty hunter!' sneered the sheriff.

'One and the same.' Duggan held the other man with a firm eye until he looked away. 'And I'm prepared to share the reward on a fifty-fifty basis.'

'Why are you being so generous?' enquired the sceptical lawdog.

'He shot my partner during the escape. So I've gotten a personal grudge to settle. The guy is desperate and will stop at nothing to get his revenge. That's why I need your back-up. But we need to move fast otherwise he might break camp before we can arrest him.'

Newcombe seemed satisfied with the explanation.

'So where is this dude camped out?' he said, unlocking the gun rack and selecting a shiny new Winchester rifle.

'I'll explain on the way,' replied Duggan. He had no intention of revealing the exact location until they were well out of town.

Evening shadows were cloaking the draw where Russ was camped when the two bushwhackers arrived. They hauled rein below the rim of a low knoll. After ground hitching their mounts, both men crept slowly up to the crest of the draw. The three-hour ride had quickly sobered the lawman who was now back to his arrogant self.

'We're in luck,' announced Duggan pointing to a hunched and blanketed form on the far side of the campfire. 'He's still here.'

Newcombe frowned.

'Turned in a mite early, ain't he?'

'Must intend to make a dawn start,' submitted his companion.

'Well, that sure as hell ain't gonna happen,' growled Newcombe. He jacked a round up the spout of the rifle.

Sighting down the barrel, he took aim and pulled the trigger. The harsh report bounced off the surrounding rocks. The lump by the fire jumped under the thudding impact of the heavy shell. A second shot ensured that the camper would stay down.

'Now let's take a look at our prize,' exulted the jubilant lawdog. Without waiting for a reply, he scuttled down the stony slope, a wide grin splitting his bluff features. Duggan followed behind, his six-shooter palmed and ready.

Newcombe toed the inert figure with his boot.

Then it struck him. There was no body, just a pile of stone. He'd been hoodwinked.

He swung on his heel.

'Drop the gun!' rapped the supposed corpse of Blackfoot Reno.

The terse command was backed up by Arby Duggan's waving pistol.

'You heard the man, floor that hogleg, or chew dirt!'

Charley Newcombe was no hero. He knew when to cut his losses. His gun hit the ground.

'You've gotten two choices here, Cimarron,' advised Russ. 'All you have to do is sign this paper and you can go free. But I warn yuh, mister,' a hard glint speared the hovering lawman. 'Show up in Del Norte again and I'll gun you down where you stand. Stoner's finished. And I aim see him penned up or lying dead on the street.' There was no compromise in the unwavering gaze.

'What does it say?' muttered the outplayed lawman,

eyeing the official-looking document.

'In short, it absolves me from any robbery and murder charge in Del Norte and lays the blame squarely in the lap of Diamond Jim Stoner.'

'You ain't blaming me for that, are yuh?' whined Newcombe.

'Sign this and you can make a clean break. Start up again someplace else.'

'What's the second choice?'

Two pistol hammers racked back to full cock. The intimation was clear. Cimarron Charley took the hint.

'Give me a pen,' he squawked.

Once the deed was accomplished, the lawman was allowed to leave. The last they heard as he galloped off was a lurid curse to return at some future date, as yet unspecified.

FIFTEEN

FACE-OFF!

A rooster crowed from one the homesteads on the edge of Del Norte. It was answered by a host of similar squawks echoing down the length of Blacktail Gulch as the new day dawned. Hungry dogs yelped, hoping to rouse their slumbering owners.

Orange and pink striations clawed back the indigo quilt wrapped around the eastern sky. But of humans there was none. Then a single figure burst from between two buildings and ran up the recently made-up street. His objective was the large house at the top of the high-class thoroughfare.

This was where all the wealthy residents of Del Norte had chosen to set down roots. And the house at the top was the grandest of all. Carved minarets and exotic spires adorned the garish mansion which sat in its own grounds; the whole estate was surrounded by a stone wall.

The bustling figure pushed open the gate and hurried up to the front door. There he hesitated. Only the foolhardy or those with urgent tidings chose to waken Diamond Jim Stoner and his new wife before nine in the morning. The man hammered on the door. He was of the latter category.

It was ten minutes before the tousle-headed mayor of Del Norte threw open the door demanding to know what all the ruckus was about.

'Best come out here and take a look, boss,' urged the Kansas Kid.

'What the hell you warblin' over?' rasped Stoner. 'This better be worth gettin' me out bed at this ungodly hour.'

Kansas stepped back and pointed to a large poster affixed to the door.

The main heading in large letters read simply: *Russ Wikeley is Back!* Underneath in a slightly smaller, though no less prominent script was the assertion: *And he's here to prove his innocence and expose the true culprit.* The rest of the text explained the details relating to the miscarriage of justice.

Stoner was dumbfounded. The unwelcome news that his nemesis had escaped from the penitentiary had not yet reached the remote settlement. Suddenly comprehending that Wikeley was back and lurking in the vicinity precipitated a cold shiver down his spine. He peered around anxiously.

'And they're pinned up all over town,' stressed the agitated gunman. 'Ain't no way the boys can pull 'em all down before the townsfolk are up.' He paused for breath then added, 'But it's the bit at the bottom you need to reckon with.'

Stoner read it out loud.

' "Russell Wikeley invites all citizens to witness the confession of Jim Stoner at noon today on Alder Street".' Only when he had finished did the full import of the threat strike home. He tried to laugh off the ridiculous nature of the allegation. But it sounded hollow in the cool light of early morn.

'Newcombe's the law around here,' blustered the gang leader. 'He oughta be able to arrest this skunk as soon as he shows his ugly mug.'

'None of the boys have seen him since yesterday morning,' declared the Kid. 'Seems like he's disappeared into thin air.'

'Or hidin' out like the drunken coward that he is,' growled Stoner. Beads of sweat coated his upper lip. He was worried. Wikeley was a smart cookie and no lightweight pushover. But Diamond Jim hadn't gotten this far without a strong backbone and the ruthless determination to stamp out all opposition.

'Get the boys together,' he rapped. 'Have them meet up at the Panhandle in an hour and we'll suss out how best to squash this rat into the dirt.'

Dewlap flopped down on to his bed in the ramshackle cabin he now occupied down by the creek. He hated the rain which constantly leaked through the tar-felted roof no matter how often he plugged the gaps.

Printing and distributing the posters to the specifications outlined by Russ had taken up much of the night. Only when the first light of dawn peeped over the serrated ridgebacks had he pinned up the last one.

There would be little chance for rest this morning. He needed to call on ex-Sheriff Ben Stockley to solicit his assistance in the forthcoming showdown. He had little doubt that Stockley would offer his wholehearted support. Stoner had ruthlessly kicked him out of office and cut his retirement pension by half.

When the old guy had complained, an alleged accident had resulted in a broken leg and a permanent limp. He knew it was Stoner's men who had precipated a horse stampede down the alley when he was walking home one evening. But there was no proof.

Jenson frowned. Four against ten hardened gunslingers were not favourable odds. Russ must have some kind of back-up plan to even out the score. A knock came on the door and his friend slipped into the cabin.

'Good work with the posters, Dewlap,' he praised the tired-looking printer. 'Once this is over you can sleep until doomsday.'

Dewlap returned the smile but it held little joviality.

'You sure this is gonna work?' he asked hesitantly.

'I ain't asking you or Stockley to go up against these critters head on,' Russ answered. 'My plan is that you conceal yourselves on either side of the street in upstairs windows. That way we've got them covered. I'm figuring that Stoner will think he's got the edge due to the small army of experienced gunnies he can call on. It'll knock the wind out of his sails when you two make your presence felt.'

'You reckon?'

Dewlap was not convinced. But he would back his friend all the way. Anything was better than having to survive on handouts from the Temperance League, and cadge drinks off celebrating prospectors.

'You betcha!' exclaimed Russ with animated zeal. 'What I'm counting on is that he hasn't reckoned with the bad feeling he's created.' He accepted a mug of sweet black coffee. 'It's not only you and Stockley who feel aggrieved. There's lots of others. Miners who have been cheated out of their rightful cut; mercantiles having to pay double rent.'

'Yeah!' cut in Jenson, displaying a new sense of optimisim and vivacity. 'And since you left, he's started a protection racket. Any storekeeper who objects suddenly finds he ain't got no goods to sell.'

'All it needs is someone to make a stand and pull everyone together.'

'And now that Newcombe's out of the frame, the law is wide open to whomsoever takes the reins,' opined Dewlap vigorously.

With renewed vigour Dewlap left the cabin to call on Stockley and determine the best place to make their stand. Russ waited for his partner to arrive. It was ten in the morning when Duggan slipped through the door. He had been forced to take a little-used back trail to avoid being spotted by any of Stoner's sentries.

Duggan had made camp close to the main trail to keep watch in the event of Charley Newcombe deciding to play a false hand.

It was just as well that the precaution had been taken.

'The sly critter doubled back,' Duggan snorted while sipping at the steaming brew he had been given. 'It was them jinglebobs he likes that gave him away. I could hear them ten minutes before he reached Indian Rock.'

Russ was all ears. 'What happened?'

'This time I didn't give the skunk a second chance.' The outlaw paused, staring into the mug of steaming brown liquid clutched in his hand. He tapped the lethal Bowie strapped to his inside leg. 'As he was passing under the overhang, I dived on him. We both crashed to the ground. But I had the edge. He was too stunned, too slow on the uptake. Old Faithful made darned sure the varmint is stoking up the fiery furnace.'

Russ gripped his partner's shoulder. 'When this is over, I'll make sure everybody knows what a solid, dependable guy you are,' he promised. 'The sheriff's job will be yours for the taking.'

'Then we better get started,' urged Duggan. 'Time stops for no man. And Jim Stoner has a date with the Devil.'

The whole town knew the score regarding the forthcoming confrontation. So when the church clock struck the noon hour, the streets were empty. Not a human soul in sight. Del Norte was like a ghost town. But behind every window facing on to Alder Street, curious eyes watched, and waited.

Tumbleweed scuttled along the edge of the broad thoroughfare, trying to seek shelter before the lid blew. A cat dashed from the cover of an alley chased by a barking dog. Then all fell silent as the bell tolled its last mournful call to combat.

Russ eased out from behind his old premises. From the far side he was joined by Arby Duggan. Tense hands covered the butts of their holstered revolvers. They stood waiting for the main act to appear.

Stoner elbowed aside the batwing doors of the Panhandle and stepped down into the street. He was accompanied by the Kansas Kid on his right, and a tall ghostly figure clad in black leather called Slug Monday to his left. Three others ranged behind.

Stoner had a wide grin pasted on his oily kisser. This was going to be a straightforward massacre. Russ Wikeley and his partner had better start praying for a decent send-off into the hereafter.

'Hold it right there, Stoner,' shouted the gruffly confident challenger. His hand clutched hold of a document, which he waved in the air. 'I have here a legally binding affidavit for you to sign.'

'And what's that all about?' came back the equally curt reply.

'I figure that don't need no explanation if'n you've read the posters scattered all over town.'

'Me and my boys don't cotton to being pushed around by escaped convicts,' snarled the gang boss. He raised his left hand. It was clearly a signal to a concealed gunman.

Stockley noticed the signal and snapped off a single

156

shot that took out one of the men standing behind Stoner. The gunman screamed once, then fell dead into a pool of water, his life blood mingling with the muddy liquid.

On the other side Dewlap Jenson, peering from an upstairs window of the hotel, had spotted a rifle poking out of the front window of the Panhandle. He cut loose with three shots in rapid-fire mode with his old Henry. Glass shattered, the rifle tumbling from nerveless fingers into the street below. Its owner followed moments later.

'Hold your fire!' The brittle holler stilled the firing. 'You didn't think me and my partner would face you off on our ownsome, did you, Stoner? We figured you'd try a crooked stunt like that. There's others in this town that want you and your kind out of the way.'

'And that includes me,' came a voice from the roof of the theatre.

'And me,' another gruff voice hollered.

Soon there were upwards of two dozen rifles aimed at Jim Stoner and his remaining gunslicks.

'Say the word, Mr Wikeley and we'll spread these skunks all over the street.'

This declaration was too much for the remaining gunmen, who dropped their weapons and surrendered.

'No more shooting!' repeated Russ, lifting his hand. 'If you men agree to quit town straight away, you can go free. And nobody will object. My quarrel ain't with the likes of you.'

A brief interlude followed as the nervous gunnies

cast anxious eyes around them. This was not the kind of reward they had been promised. Individual upsurges in defiance could easily be handled. But when a whole town decided to challenge the status quo, that was too much. Hired gunslingers always needed an edge. It was the only way to grow old in their game.

'You got a deal,' came back the response.

'Dirty double-crossing scum,' growled the Kansas Kid. Swinging abruptly on his heel, he drilled the speaker plumb in the centre of the forehead. 'That's what happens to rats that betray—'

He never got to finish the sentence. A myriad guns blasted. The Kid's body, leaking blood from a dozen punctures, was tossed around like a flag in the wind.

Only Jim Stoner and his most recently hired gun were left standing. Slug Monday's stony mask slipped. The lean hardcase was made of sterner stuff. Yet even he knew when the chips were down.

'Sorry Mr Stoner,' he said, raising his hands. 'This sure ain't my fight.' He backed away gingerly so as not to incite a further volley of lethal gunfire.

'Damn cowardly skunk!' howled the frustrated mayor.

Russ walked slowly towards the isolated gang leader, who now looked forlorn and deserted. He holstered his gun.

'It's come down to you and me, Stoner.' His voice remained low, almost casual. Yet to those watching it throbbed with menacing intensity, and left no room for compromise. Then he called out to all those watching from their places of concealment. 'I want no interference,' he said. 'This is between me and him. Winner takes all!'

Arby Duggan stood to one side, but kept his gun cocked and ready, just in case.

Silence descended on Del Norte's main drag. Seconds dragged by, time held no meaning as everyone held their breath.

Then it happened. In a blur of movement that nobody could later recall, Stoner went for his gun. Bullets flew. White smoke from ratcheting six-shooters filled the static air. Nobody moved as the swirling tendrils slowly dispersed to leave the last man standing.

Russ Wikeley emerged from the swirling haze and walked slowly towards his sworn enemy. There was blood on his left arm. But it was only a scratch. Stoner lay dead in the middle of the street.

It was over. Del Norte would sleep peacefully tonight.

A shadow quickly left the confines of the Panhandle saloon and rushed to his side.

'I'm glad you won,' gushed the plaintive voice of someone who was clinging to his side. 'That awful critter deserved to die after all he's put this town through.'

Russ brushed the girl aside. An acerbic look of disdain darkened the handsome visage. Eleanor Harding stepped into a rut and fell over. Streaks of mud coated the expensive green satin-brocade dress specially imported from Chicago. Guffaws of delight from the emerging bystanders accompanied the inadvertent tumble.

159

Russ's stoic demeanour remained immutable.

'You've made your bed.' His voice was flat, the sentiment brief and to the point. 'Now lie in it. I don't expect it'll be empty for long.' Then he turned towards his horse and mounted up.

'Town's all yours now, Arby,' he said addressing his partner with a more breezy outlook. A sly wink followed. 'I've got me an appointment that can't keep.'

'Good luck to yuh, buddy,' murmured the reformed outlaw as Russ Wikeley nudged his cayuse down the street.

At long last it was over. Reparation had been achieved and his good name restored. The rider's thoughts were now fixed on a vision of loveliness awaiting him on the banks of the White River.